PRAISE FOR THE WORKS OF
SHELDON HIGDON

DARK ROOTS

"Sheldon Higdon takes us down some shadowy roads with *Dark Roots*! This creepy thriller takes weird, wild, and shocking twists and turns. Grab this!" —Jonathan Maberry, *New York Times* bestselling author of *Red Empire* and *Ghosts of the Void*

"This is a nasty coiled-up snake of a novel with plenty of venom in its bite." —Four-time Bram Stoker Award-winning author Tim Waggoner

"A journey through the twisted and macabre mind of human depravity." —Nora B. Peevy for *Hellnotes*

"Sheldon Higdon's *Dark Roots* is a deeply disturbing and brilliantly twisted read. Blending the haunting psychological depth of *True Detective*, the relentless tension of *To Catch a Killer*, and the eerie dread of *The Black Phone*, this story grips from the first page and never lets go. It's a nightmarish descent into darkness that will make every parent's skin crawl and stomach turn. A solid 5 Shovels read!" —Thom Erb, author of *Snow Black*, *The Last in Line*, and *Heaven, Hell, or Houston*

"The twists keep coming! Mysterious family secrets. Small town tragedy. Revelations hidden in the walls. *Dark Roots* has a little bit of everything for those who like their crime fiction dark. It's a page turner all the way through!" —Corey Farrenkopf, author of *Living in Cemeteries* and *Haunted Ecologies*

"Multilayered and multifaceted, *Dark Roots* never stops twisting the blade of evil surprises and terrible revelation." —William Holloway, author of *Lucky's Girl* and *Blackwood Estates*

THE EERIE BROTHERS AND THE WITCHES OF AUTUMN

"Sheldon Higdon delivers a fun, freaky, and frightening novel—first in what I hope is a long series—for young readers. It's *Goosebumps* meets *Supernatural*." —Jonathan Maberry, *New York Times* bestselling author of *Rot & Ruin* and editor of *Don't Turn Out the Lights*

"*The Eerie Brothers and the Witches of Autumn* is a fast-paced adventure through time with the perfect touch of Halloween esthetic and humor in this creepy fun middle grade novel about discovering who you are, and the importance of protecting family and friends you can count on." — Darcy Marks, author of *Grounded For All Eternity*

"A great addition to the MG canon of books about magic and witches." —Aric Cushing, author of *Vampire Boy* and screenwriter of the feature film *There's No Such Thing As Vampires*

"Author Higdon is a talented word weaver with a deep comprehension of his characters and a vividly expressed imagination." —The Haunted Reading Room

ANTHOLOGIES

Horror Library, Vol. 8: "We Can't Let Go"

"We Can't Let Go" by Sheldon Higdon—a very eerie troubling tale of a social worker who meets a child and their mother. The encounter is from the off immediately, not feeling right, but then Sheldon adds an even darker dimension. Pure horror." —Runalong TheShelves.net

"...grotesquerie occurs in "We Can't Let Go" by Sheldon Higdon, a gruesome exploration of motherly bonds with a Richard Matheson–esque final twist." —TheBedlamFiles.com

"In the deeply unsettling "We Can't Let Go" by Sheldon Higdon, a social worker visits a weird woman and her son with a shocking result." —HorrorTree.com

Tales from the Lake, Vol. 4: "Drowning in Sorrow"

"...the story is so beautifully written, and so heartfelt, and the character evolution is so seamless. A terribly beautiful and beautifully terrible tale, this is one of my favourites in this volume." —Reading Reindeer, Goodreads Review

Death, Be Not Proud: "Where the Dead Go to Die"

"Sheldon Higdon has written a short story titled "Where the Dead Go to Die," which has been placed on the HWA Stoker Recommended Reading List. As soon as I started reading it, I realized something. This is not your normal zombie story. It's weird, it's creepy, it's freaking twisted, but it also rocks. Watch out, my fellow writer friends, Sheldon knows how to get into our minds and twist our neurons, so they spark, sending us into his crazy world with some great story telling. I must warn you; this can be visually disturbing. Hehehehe! Two bony thumbs up from the evil little jester and myself." —Charles Day (Author & Owner of Evil Jester Press)

DARK ROOTS

SHELDON HIGDON

JOURNALSTONE
YOUR LINK TO ARTIST TALENT

ISBN: 978-1-68510-170-1 (trade paper)
ISBN: 978-1-68510-171-8 (ePub)
The Library of Congress Control Number has been applied for.

First printing edition: November 14, 2025
Published by JournalStone Publishing in the United States of America.
Cover Design: Mikio Murakami
Edited by Sean Leonard
Proofreading and Cover/Interior Layout by Scarlett R. Algee

JournalStone Publishing
1400 North Wood Rd.
Murphysboro, IL 62966

JournalStone books may be ordered through booksellers or by contacting:
JournalStone | www.journalstone.com

To Seton Hill University, without which this book wouldn't exist.

DARK ROOTS

CHAPTER ONE

Erie, Pennsylvania. October 31, 1989.

Little Superman squeezed his mother's hand as a flock of ghouls and goblins sped toward them. "Hello, Ms. Fletcher," one of the masked kids said. "Happy Halloween!" another said as they disappeared into the night and then reappeared down the road beneath the glow of a streetlamp.

"Remember, Travis, you can't have any candy until I go through it," the hero's mother said.

Travis shook his pillowcase. "I got a bunch."

"Yep." She smiled down at him. "And let's hope you don't get a bunch of cavities."

"I can't get cavities."

"Oh, and why not?"

"Cuz I'm Superman!" He ran in circles with one arm straight out, red cape flapping behind him.

"Okay, okay," his mother laughed. "Let's get home and show Daddy your candy before you defeat the evils of tooth decay."

"Excuse me, ma'am?"

Travis and his mother spun around to a red wagon. A kind of car Travis had never seen before, especially one that was so sneaky.

"You about scared us to death," she said. "I didn't hear you pull up."

The driver's face was concealed by a wolf mask.

Travis stepped behind his mother's legs and grabbed her hand.

"Mommy," he whispered.

"I'm sorry," the wolf's muffled voice said. "Wasn't my intention, I assure you."

"Can I help you?" she said.

"Have you seen a little girl with blonde pigtails running around here? Actually, Little Red Riding Hood. Wearing a red shawl? You can't miss her. About eight years old."

"I'm sorry, but I haven't seen her."

Travis poked his head out from behind his mother.

"Hey there, Superman," the wolf said. A ratty flannel sleeve reached out, and a finger pointed toward Travis. "Maybe *you* can help me find her. After all, you have powers, don't you?"

Travis vanished behind her legs.

"Wish I could be more helpful," she said.

"Cute boy you got there," the wolf said, "and thank you." He coasted away and turned left at the end of the road.

Travis stepped out from behind her and shivered from the October air. Something flapped overhead and landed in a nearby tree. Leaves rustled. His mother stared down the street into the darkness where the wagon had turned. "Hope he finds her," she said. "C'mon, let's go home and check your candy."

They came to a stop at the corner where the old car had turned. Several masked kids, laughing and yelling, ran across the street. Up against a thicket of shrubs and trees, the wagon sat on the side of the road with its headlights out. Silver moonlight cast broken shadows across it—and walking toward Travis and his mother, the wolf with a crowbar in hand. Along with his tattered flannel shirt, he wore jeans with holes in the knees. At that moment, Travis wished he could fly. His stomach twisted. His heart beat like a baseball card flicking in the spokes of his bicycle's wheel.

Travis wrapped his arms around his mother's thigh.

"It's okay, dear." She rubbed his head.

"This isn't my night. It seems I'm having some car trouble." The wolf turned, pointed toward the wagon, and removed his mask. "Gets hot beneath this thing." He smiled. "Got a flat tire on the passenger side. I can fix it, but I need someone to hold my flashlight. Could you assist me?"

"We really need to get home," she said. "It's getting late."

"It'll only take a minute," he said. "Please. The sooner I can fix it, the sooner I can find my little girl. I'm sure my wife's worried to pieces. And so am I. I wouldn't bother you, but..."

"Having a little one myself, I'd be devastated if something happened to him."

Travis tugged at her arm.

"It'll be all right, sweetie." She picked up Travis and followed the man to his wagon.

"I wanna go home."

"Right after this we'll go home and eat some of your candy, okay?"

The red wagon's back gate sat open. No interior light glowed.

She set Travis down. "You got a flashlight?"

"I do. Let me check the front."

The man stopped at the back gate and tossed in his wolf mask while she and Travis stood in the moonlight. He hopped in the front and searched.

"Mister?" she said. "Did you find it?"

Two large boxes sat inside the wagon, and she leaned in for a closer look.

"You'll find nothing in there but stacks of encyclopedias," the man said, standing behind them, his face lit by the beam of a flashlight.

She swirled around. "Uh, I'm… I didn't mean to—"

"That's quite all right," he said, kneeling before Travis. "Do you like books, Superman?"

Travis looked up at his mom.

"It's all right. You can answer him."

"My mommy reads me bedtime stories."

"Would you like a new book? One that will teach you things?" He looked up. "Like the stars above." And then returned to Travis. "But first you have to ask your mommy."

"We couldn't," she said. "Thank you anyway."

"Encyclopedias are knowledge," he said, standing. "Don't want to keep your boy from learning, do you?"

"That's nice of you, but I couldn't."

"It's on me. And if I had your boy, I wouldn't pass up the offer."

"Well, if you're offering."

"I am. Go ahead and take one."

She sat Travis on the gate of the wagon, opened a box, and pulled out an encyclopedia. Its spine was frayed, loose threads splaying about.

The man handed Travis the flashlight. "This will make for better reading."

"I think we're going to need that," she said.

"We'll just have to use the moonlight. I'd rather your son have it."

Travis aimed the beam of light at his mom's back and followed her to the front of the car. When she looked back at him, he shined it in her face. "I can't see, sweetie. Go ahead and look at the book the nice man gave you."

Travis opened it and flipped through its pages. Crickets chirped from somewhere close by. From the front of the wagon, his mom said, "This tire isn't flat. What are—?"

The wagon shook. A crack like the sound of walnuts being broken open by Travis' Uncle Leonard on Christmas Eve grabbed his attention. Another crack followed. This one was softer, wetter, as if watermelon had hit the pavement.

His heart beat in his throat. "Mommy." He swallowed hard.

Turning to climb down from the gate, he stopped when the light of his flashlight shone a pair of work boots. Travis raised it up to the man's face, which was now streaked with what looked like red paint. He screamed and dropped the flashlight onto the street. The man pushed him, slamming him into the boxes, the encyclopedia flying in with him. Travis' back shot with pain where the corner of a box jabbed him. His eyes watered. The man smiled and slammed the gate, then locked it. He slid into the driver's seat, and the engine roared to life. Its headlights flicked on.

"Where's my mommy?"

"Quiet!"

"I want my mommy!"

"Your mommy can't help you!"

"I wanna go home!"

"Do you?"

"Yes!" cried Travis.

"Get into the back seat. You do that, *maybe*I'll take you home."

Travis looked at him through teary eyes. The man appeared wavy, like when Travis first swam underwater at the YMCA and his mommy's legs were all bendy. He wiped his eyes. A dark figure with the face of a wolf came into view.

"Now!"

Travis crawled over the boxes and slipped onto the back seat, legs underneath him. He grabbed the door handle and shook it.

"The doors won't be of any use, Superman," said the man's muffled voice from behind his mask. "I made sure of it."

The wagon moved forward and thumped over something. Travis looked out his window and there lay the upper half of his mother's body spotlighted—from somewhere beneath the wagon—by the flashlight. Blood pooled all around her lifeless face.

Travis screamed. She looked frozen, eyes unmoving. No words came to his young mind at the sight of her. Only a quick memory. A snapshot of the time when they played the staring contest during supper. Even though he had won, her face wore the same expression as it did now. Travis didn't like it, and something about it made his throat tighten and his stomach sour. The wagon thumped again. He kicked the back of the driver's seat, and then tried the door handle again, jerking it back and forth. It gave no hope of escape. He felt for the window handle but found nothing. Travis pounded on the glass with his fists and bawled.

"If you don't stop then I'll tie you up too."

Travis stopped. His hands hurt. He breathed heavy as he trembled. Travis didn't know what to do. He was scared, confused. Images of his mother flashed through his head. Of her smiling face. Of her laughing. Of her goodnight kisses. Of her frozen face. His chest hurt. His heart hurt. Warm tears slid down his face. He stomped onto the floor and heard a *humpf!* He wiped his face with his blue sleeve, looked down, and saw something move, but it was too dark to tell what it was.

"You wanna see your new friend?" Without looking, the wolf reached over the seat with one arm, flicked a flame from a lighter, and lowered it near the floor.

The orange glow fell upon a little blonde girl of about eight years old, her ankles and arms tied behind her. Mouth gagged. A red shawl ripped and draped over her. Her dirty cheeks streaked with tears.

"Mommy," whispered Travis.

The man flipped the lighter shut and drove on as Travis buried his wet face into his hands and cried.

CHAPTER TWO

Benjamin Cole sat on the edge of his desk, tapping a pen against his thigh, and faced the twelve college students standing around, talking to one another in his Journalism 101 class. He glanced at his wristwatch. One more hour, and he would be out of here for summer break.

"Okay, looks like you're all here. And if you're not, then you're smarter than the rest of us." Laughter filled the room. He marked a sheet of paper and laid it next to him. "Today's the big day." He parked the pen behind his ear. "Not only because it's the last class of the semester before summer break, but also because I need to turn all of your articles in to the school newspaper. If we don't turn them in today, the school newspaper won't run your pieces in the fall." He hopped off his desk. "So, I want you guys and gals to pair up with your writing partner and when I call you, I want you to bring up your article. Good? Good."

The students shuffled about the room as he sat behind his desk.

"First up, Joann and Bella."

Joann, who wore a t-shirt with the words *Point Park University* on it, led the way. She brushed her curly hair to the side as Bella handed Benjamin their article.

"Here you go, Mr. Cole," Bella's round face split into a smile, which revealed a small gap between her front teeth.

Benjamin took it from her and leaned forward in his chair. "The closing of the Braddock Hospital, right?"

He could barely remember who had what assignment anymore. He was lucky he remembered his students' names. After teaching journalism for so long, the stories and faces all melded together. Every semester he ran through the motions. Speak, read, grade, report.

"Yes," Joann said.

"Did you gals edit this down to seven hundred words? Can't be over."

"Wasn't easy, but yeah," Bella said. "Even checked the spelling again."

"Good. And you rechecked your sources? Facts?" He held up their article. "There's no room for error, and there's especially no room for fiction."

"Like a billion times," Joann said.

"Okay. Take your seats." Benjamin stood with the girls' article still in his hand. "Class."

The students looked up in unison, except for Chuck Gullen, who fiddled around with his shoelaces. Joann and Bella took their seats.

"Remember." Benjamin waved the paper in the air. "I'm handing in your work just as you turn it in to me. I assume, and expect, that you rechecked your work for spelling, et cetera. Your facts are straight. You're reporting the news. So your work should be serious and so should you. Got it?"

The students responded with a mixture of nods and "Yes, Mr. Cole."

Benjamin sat back down, laying the paper on his desk. "Jerry and Richard, you're up."

Jerry's rotund frame waddled up to Benjamin's desk with papers in his hand, while Richard followed with his straw-like hair sticking out from beneath his *Pioneers* ball cap.

"You guys did your piece on…uh…"

"The Whitmore Case," Jerry said.

"Yes," Benjamin said. "The child-killing father. What do you guys plan on doing since this story is ongoing? With court appearances, continual police investigations, and so on?" Jerry raised his finger and was about to say something when Benjamin said, "Richard?"

"Uh, well, we'll have to stay on top of it, of course, like flies on butter."

Without hesitation, Jerry said, "Yeah, I don't see why the paper wouldn't take a follow-up next semester. I'll have to make callbacks to the Whitmore family and hit them harder. Y'know, 'How will you move on since your husband murdered your only child?' Or 'How does it feel to have been married to someone who turned out to not only be a killer but a total stranger?' The nitty gritty stuff."

The ugly face of journalism. Its jagged, earth-stained teeth ready for the bite. If you don't intrude into a poor woman's life and get the scoop, you don't sell papers.

Jerry added, "Can I retitle it?"

"Next time have your title squared away. I'll allow it though," Benjamin said. "Is that okay with you, Richard?"

Richard shrugged. "Sounds cool to me."

"Change it from 'Dad Kills Son' to 'Family Stranger,'" Jerry said.

How appropriate.

As of late, Benjamin felt like a stranger in his relationship with Aisha. It had become strained. This was something they had dealt with before, but for a different reason. When he and Aisha Jones first started dating, they were both stressed out because a few of their friends didn't like the fact that he was white and she was black. Those friends were let go for obvious reasons. Now, the anxiety came from her want of a family, and since he didn't share her feelings about kids, he became the stranger between them. More and more they fought about marriage and children, and more and more he tried to ignore the subject.

"Okay." Benjamin jotted down the new title on a piece of paper. "I'll make the change."

Not sure I can make the change with Aisha, though.

? ? ?

The halls of Point Park University weren't carved out of fancy marble from Italy or exotic wood from South America. They were basic, and Benjamin liked it that way. He crossed the glass-enclosed bridge over Wood Street that connected Lawrence Hall to Academic Hall like an umbilical cord.

The Last Mile.

In reality, it was about fifty feet long, nothing near an actual mile. Still, he gave it the name because it was the last section of his walk before heading down the stairs and out the door for his much-needed summer break.

To a waiting argument? I hope not. I hope the summer doesn't break us apart.

"Mister Cole!"

Richard's voice came from behind Benjamin and he glanced over his shoulder to his student waving his arm. He stopped on the first few steps of the main stairway that led down to a pair of glass doors. His summer break was in sight.

"Mister Cole." Richard straightened his hat. "I just wanted to tell you that I really enjoyed taking your Journalism 101 course this term."

Benjamin jerked back. "You did?"

"Surprised?"

"I am. I didn't think you were interested in it."

"I know I haven't showed it much," Richard removed his hat, combed his fingers through his dirty-blond hair, and replaced it on his head, "but I have."

"Well, thanks. I'm glad you liked it. I'll, uh, see you in September. I gotta run." Benjamin turned to finish the last remaining steps.

"I'm actually thinking about switching my major after taking your course."

The last few steps to freedom.

"Never thought I'd ever consider journalism as a major," Richard said.

"It's still early to switch." Benjamin stepped down a step. The glass doors were closer, but so far away. "Really, I've gotta run." He took a few more steps. "I'll see you next semester."

"Not if I see you first." Richard chuckled.

Benjamin bounded down the last few steps and pushed through the doors, out into the warm air. A car horn beeped.

A silver Prius pulled alongside him, holding up traffic as Benjamin slid into the passenger seat. He latched his seatbelt, closed his eyes, and released a sigh. From behind him, a big wet tongue licked his cheek.

"Aww, Hogarth kissed you hello. Now can your girlfriend give you one too?" Benjamin opened an eye and looked over at Aisha sitting behind the steering wheel. She smiled at him.

"I guess one won't hurt," he said. "C'mere, Hogarth." He turned back, expecting to wrap his arm around the large head of an English Mastiff. Instead, Hogarth leaned back, squished next to a child's car seat, and stared out the window as drool gathered around his jowls.

Aisha hit Benjamin on the arm and leaned over to kiss him on the cheek when a car horn blasted. A man's voice screamed obscenities from behind them while he shook his fist out his driver's window. Aisha pressed a button on the control panel of her door and raised her window.

"He's just jealous because you got such a hottie of a woman."

The man sped by, honking his horn.

"Now, where's that kiss?" Benjamin pulled her over to him.

"Not on the lips." She winked. "That'll come later."

She pressed her full lips against his cheek and held them there for a minute. They were soft against his skin like the silky feel of a flower petal.

Aisha pulled back. "Ben?"

"Yeah."

"Who's the crazy-eyed kid watching us?"

Benjamin turned to Richard standing in the middle of the sidewalk with a big grin on his face. He raised his hand and gave Benjamin a thumbs-up like Fonzi giving Ritchie his approval of a hot girl.

"You're supposed to be a guard dog, Hogarth," Aisha said.

Benjamin nodded at Richard and said, "Let's go."

During the ride home he rested his eyes for most of the way, opening them somewhere along Route 28. He stretched his long frame as best he could in the matchbox of a car.

"Welcome to the living, Mr. Cole," Aisha said.

"I wasn't asleep. Just resting my eyes."

"So, you never told me how your day went."

"Slow and," he released a long yawn, "slower."

"And you didn't need to bring anything home with you?"

"Nah, all I had to do was sanitize my office and classroom."

Aisha glanced into her side mirror. "You make it sound like it's full of germs or something."

"You're not a germ." Benjamin poked her on the leg and held up his finger. "See, no cooties."

"If I were a germ, we wouldn't be together. I'd be dating some other handsome white guy." Aisha gave a quick look back at Hogarth. "And I'd have a ring on my finger."

Didn't even make it home before she brought it up. I either load my barrels for a comeback or avoid the gunfight altogether.

"You staying over tonight?" Benjamin said.

"Can't." She flipped the turn signal on and turned onto a bridge crossing over a river. "I have to get my bags packed for tomorrow morning's flight."

"Stay tonight, and then I'll help you tomorrow. We'll get breakfast and head to your place after." Benjamin slid his hand across her tight jeans and squeezed her inner thigh. "We'll have a little Saturday morning snuggle time." He arched his eyebrows and gave her his best puppy-dog eyes.

"I can't. I'd love too, really. Besides, you're not the only one getting out for summer, y'know? I've gotta pick up Darren from school and take him to Carol's. As usual, his deadbeat dad is too *busy* for his son. Asshole."

"C'mon. Do they really *need* the coordinator of Special Music Programs at the conference? I'm sure Carnegie Mellon University will do just fine without you. Can't you just send someone else in your place instead?"

"I don't have the authority." She laid her hand on top of his. "And yeah, I need to be there."

"You're still going to take a few days off to spend with me, aren't you?"

They pulled up in front of a two-story cedar-shingled house with a veranda that ran along its front. Aisha threw the car into park.

"Of course," she said, turning toward him in her seat.

"Wish I could go to conferences and hang out, and at the university's expense to boot." Benjamin flipped down his visor and looked at Hogarth in its mirror. "Isn't that right, buddy? Wanna go on a trip?" Hogarth stared at him, panting, his thick tongue hanging out of his mouth.

"Sounds like you're jealous," she said. "And Hogarth will keep you company while I'm gone."

"What about the kiss you promised earlier?" Benjamin flipped up the visor and raised an eyebrow at Aisha.

In his peripheral vision, Benjamin saw Hogarth shake his square head, sending thick mucus in all directions. Aisha ducked, but he wasn't quick enough. He rubbed his face. A long string of sticky ooze ran across his cheek and onto the rim of his glasses. Aisha looked at him and started laughing. Hogarth released a thunderous bark and wagged his tail so hard it sounded like a bullwhip hitting the backseat of the tiny car.

"Ask and you shall receive," she said, her hand covering her laughter.

"He slimed me." Benjamin took off his glasses. "You got a Kleenex or something? A beach towel?"

Aisha giggled as she pulled out a tissue from her leopard-print handbag and handed it to him. "I'm sorry," she said, zipping her bag back up. "It's not like he hasn't slobbered you before."

"I know, but this one's the worst yet. I had nowhere to run." Benjamin wiped his glasses off and returned them to his face. He folded the tissue and wiped his cheek clean. "Well, like you said, at least I got some sort of kiss. Better than nothing."

"You want me to kiss you and make you all better?"

"Y'know what? I'm not in the mood for a kiss after all. Hogarth has satisfied my libido, and later, I think we'll snuggle. Right, buddy?"

"Oh, c'mon now." She pulled him close and bit his upper lip, tugging on it.

After two years of dating, her tenderness and confidence still crippled him. No matter the recent arguments, the scent of her vanilla perfume and the soft curls of her sable hair caused him to melt into his seat.

After a few moments, she pulled away. "How's that?"

"Huh?"

"That's what I thought."

"You really can't stay?" he finally said.

"Wish I could."

"Fine, how about dinner then? You have to eat."

"Dinner I can do." She smiled. "What are you making?"

"Uh, I thought of ordering Chinese." He stepped out and flipped his seat forward so Hogarth could exit the car. "Or pizza."

"I'll go get Chinese." She put the car into gear. "Your usual?"

"Of course." He pushed the seat back, shut the door, and waved as she did a U-turn and drove away.

???

After Benjamin fed Hogarth, he left him a large bone to chew on while he entered his office, which was the living room, and turned on his laptop that called the top of a foldable TV tray home. It had been a long time since Benjamin felt as if he had something to look forward to, something to work on besides grading papers or writing articles on spec for freelance projects. Journalism, he thought, was getting redundant. How many times could he write about some tragedy that happened downtown to some poor soul? He was tired of asking inappropriate and insensitive questions to people.

How do you feel about losing your father and everything you own? Ridiculous.

While on summer break, he decided he would try his hand at writing fiction. A novel. Maybe it was the outlet he needed to feel passionate about writing again. Or teaching. Maybe it would open up a new career. Either way, the challenge would be good.

He took a seat on a small chair and clicked open MS Word on his laptop. At the top of the new page, he wrote, *In Deception*, then hit the *enter* key, spaced down a few lines, and wrote, *Chapter One*. But before he could put in his earphones and listen to music while he wrote, a knock came from the front door.

Hogarth came barking into the room. Benjamin grabbed him by the collar and struggled to hold him back. "Sit!" He opened the door while trying to handle the large dog. Hogarth barked with excitement, his tail slapping at the air. Benjamin let go of the collar and said, "This is a surprise."

CHAPTER THREE

With ten years of experience on the force, Detective Eddie Lane was still the rookie among his brothers. It didn't matter, because he was good at his job and he took it seriously. And for that, his coworkers respected him for it.

He dipped his vanilla biscotti into his warm tea as he sat on a wrought-iron bench in front of the station and took in the morning traffic. Waddling down the sidewalk toward him was Detective Carl Smallman, a short and rotund man whose head was two hairs away from being completely bald. Crammed beneath the armpit of his suit jacket was a brown paper bag. In one thick hand he held a paper cup while in the other he was munching on a donut.

"Hey, Ed." Crumbs fell from his mouth. "You hear about that two-year-old kid being kidnapped yesterday? Was taken from a daycare. You believe that? A freakin' daycare."

"Really? No, I didn't hear about that." Eddie took a bite of his Italian cookie. "Is there an Amber Alert out?"

"Yeah. Nowhere is safe these days, huh? Man."

"Crazy, that's for sure."

"Yup. You got the time?"

"When are you going to buy a watch?" Eddie checked his wristwatch. "Quarter to eight."

"Haven't had one for fifty-three years. Why start now?" He placed the uneaten portion in his mouth and held out the brown bag. "Donut?"

Eddie raised an eyebrow at him."When's the last time you've seen me eating a donut? I don't want to add to the stereotype any more than is needed." He held up his biscotti. "I'm fine, thanks."

"Hell, I started the stereotype." Carl rolled the top of the bag closed and tucked it under his arm."Anyway, I better get in there. Thanks for the time."

"Welcome."

Eddie often wondered how he ended up working in Oakmont, a small town outside of Pittsburgh. Not that he really didn't understand how he got here, he was from the 'Burgh, but he wondered if he could up and move to a larger city where he could run with the big boys. Cities like New York or Chicago, maybe even Los Angeles. The only crimes in Oakmont were speeding tickets or weekend drunks. He took a sip of tea and checked his watch. Eight o'clock. He ate the last bite of his biscotti and went inside the station to start his day.

???

"Since Officer Tremblay is out sick and Officer Earl is on vacation in the Bahamas, it looks like we're covering calls," Eddie said as he and Carl walked toward an unmarked Malibu in the station's lot.

"I could use a vacation myself," Carl said.

"Me too. How about you drive the first half of the shift and I'll drive the second?"

Carl held up his coffee cup and a half-eaten glazed donut in response.

"Never mind, I'll drive the first half."

"Much obliged."

Both men climbed in and Eddie started the car, backed up, and pulled out of the lot.

They drove around town and then out to the Oakmont Heights Golf Course followed by a drive out to the Dark Hollow Woods Park and finished up the first part of the day by passing the Pittsburgh Zoo. All the while, Carl talked Eddie's ear off about his wife who—by her account—wouldn't get off his ass about fixing the garage door and that *she* should've taken her mother's advice those thirty years ago and married a man more able and stable. Eddie heard his personal problems before, the whole force had, but this vent was of new information, and rather than cutting him off, he listened. After some time, Carl said nothing more. Maybe he exposed himself too much and felt embarrassed.

"Hungry? It's been a few hours," Eddie said. "We could get some burgers at the Oakmont Cafe?"

"Sure," Carl patted his large stomach. "I could fuel up."

???

While working on his fries, Eddie said, "Question."

Carl sipped his Coke, released a small belch, and said, "Shoot."

"You ever wish you worked in a bigger city?"

"Like New York or something?"

"Yeah." Eddie took a small bite of his burger.

"Nope." Carl dipped a few fries into a puddle of ketchup on his plate, ate them, and wiped the grayish caterpillar on his upper lip with a napkin. "I like my danger simple. Speeders, jaywalkers, and noise complaints are all this guy needs and wants. No thanks, New York."

"So the calls about the Peeping Tom in the park are fine with you?"

"Rather a Peeping Tom than a Hillside Strangler."

"True. Or some father killing his son. Did you hear about that?"

"Yeah. Sicko," Carl said. "Let the Picksburgh police handle those ones."

Eddie chuckled.

"What?"

"I still laugh whenever I hear your roots slip out. Your Pittsburghese."

"Roots? You're from here, y'know?"

"Got me there." He laughed. "Just never picked up the dialect. Too young, maybe."

"Give it another year and I'll have you saying Stillers and Dahntahnn'at."

"More like ten."

A waitress in her early thirties, red hair pulled back into a ponytail, paused at their table. "What, you don't like the way we talk?" She held a bowl of salad in one hand and a glass of water in the other. Her freckled face wore little makeup and a big smile.

"No, I uh… I mean…" Eddie stumbled over his words. She was beautiful and his tongue didn't help him.

"What my partner is trying to say is what time do you get off?"

The waitress giggled.

"Is that what you're saying?"

"Carl." Eddie gave him a stern look. "I was just…"

"I better take this salad to my customer before it gets cold." She smiled and winked at Eddie, then walked away to a booth where a woman with a teenage girl was sitting.

???

Back inside the cruiser, Carl said, "Might want to work on your *game*, my friend."

"Why'd you do that? Put me on the spot?"

"Let me ask you a personal question."

"Fire away," Eddie said. "Wait. How personal?"

"Besides your lack of skills in picking up women, why haven't you ever gotten married? I can't recall the last time I heard you talk about a girlfriend."

"Ah, *that* personal." Eddie chuckled. "It's hard to find, uh, *someone* that's willing to wonder, on an almost nightly basis, if their husband, or boyfriend, will make it home from a shift. Not sure if I could expect that."

"I guess that's admirable of you," Carl said. "Hell, when I get home from late shifts, the wife's sawing logs. Not a care in her bones."

"Can I ask you a question?"

"I'm all ears," Carl said.

"No disrespect, but why have you stayed with her all these years?"

"Too old to start over," Carl said.

The answer was straight to the point and simple. Eddie didn't expect it. He thought he'd get more of a rant like the one he heard earlier. Without letting Carl see his stare, he watched him fidget in his seat.

"And don't ask about kids. She never wanted any, and I didn't have a say. I just wanted *one*, y'know?"

Eddie nodded.

Carl cleared his throat. "Anyways, I think the waitress we had was around your age. You could always hit her up when the time comes."

"Yeah, I could."

In front of them, a black Denali swerved over the center line, back to the right lane, and then over the center line again.

"What do we have here?" Carl said.

Eddie snatched the CB and called to the dispatcher.

"This is C-16. Seems I have a possible DUI on Third Avenue. I need a rundown on a plate."

"C-16. Go ahead."

"Daniel. Alpha. Knoxville. Niner. One. Seven. Three. Over."

"It's not even the weekend and we already have a boozer," Carl said.

"Appears that way."

"C-16. No priors or standings. Do you request back-up?"

"Negative. C-16 out."

"Light 'em up," Carl said.

Eddie flipped a switch on the dashboard then flicked a lever on his steering wheel. Loud bursts echoed outside the cruiser.

The SUV pulled over to the side of the road.

"It's all yours," Carl said. "I'll hit the other side of the truck for passengers."

Eddie closed his eyes and inhaled, held it for a few seconds, and exhaled.

"Still having anxiety?" Carl said. "Thought by now that would've been cured."

"I just can't shake it. Every time I'm about to put myself on the line, I get all nervous."

"It's not like this is your first DUI. You're a ten-year veteran and not once has anything happened to you. This is why the guys rib you. No offense, but I can't see you working in New York. Just do what you always do and stay focused on the scene at hand. Last thing you ever want is to let your worries get the best of you. Could cost you big time. Don't hesitate, just act."

"I know," Eddie said, and with that, he climbed out and eased his way to the truck's driver's side. Carl took slow steps toward the passenger door.

The truck remained idling.

Its windows were tinted, so Eddie couldn't get a clear view of whether a man or a woman was behind the wheel. He stopped a few feet from the car door and yelled, "Driver! Cut your engine!"

The engine died.

"Driver. Now roll down your window and put both hands out where I can see them."

Nothing happened.

"Driver?"

Eddie pulled his sidearm, aiming it downward.

"Driver! Roll your window down and put both of your hands out where I can see them! Now!"

From the other side of the SUV, Carl's voice bellowed, "I got visual on one person."

"Driver, I'm telling you one last—"

The driver's window lowered and two pasty hands appeared into the open.

"Why-why you pullin' a—a gun on me?" a voice slurred.

"Is there anyone else in your vehicle?" Eddie said.

"Un-uh."

"Do you have any weapons in your vehicle or on your person?"

"Nope."

"Slowly, with your right hand, I want you to open the door and climb out. Slowly. Keep your left hand out the window where I can see it. Understood?"

"Th-this a test?"

"Understood?" Eddie said.

"Yeah, yeah."

"Go ahead and get out."

A hand disappeared from view and the door opened. Out came a man wearing a Steelers jersey with palms raised above his head.

"Turn around and place your hands on the side of your truck and part your legs. Understood?"

The man stumbled backward. "Yes, sir." He turned and placed both hands flat against the SUV and parted his legs.

Carl came around with cuffs in his hand. "Just in case."

Eddie holstered his firearm.

"Would you mind if we took a look inside your vehicle?" Carl said.

"Alllll yours."

Carl went to the cab and climbed in.

From his back pocket, Eddie pulled out a pair of rubber gloves.

"Do you have anything sharp or pointy on you that might stick me or cut me? Needles or a knife?"

"Nothing."

Eddie patted the man down. "How many drinks have you had today?"

"Mmmm." The man squinted and held up five fingers. "Two?"

Carl hopped out of the cab. "I'd say close to a case by the looks of it."

"You can turn around." Eddie handed Carl the man's wallet. "Looks like you were having a bit of a party in your truck."

"Something like that," the man said.

Carl searched through the wallet, pulled out a driver's license, and studied it.

"Y'know, it's against the law to drink while you drive, Mr. Price," Carl said.

"Tyson. And I know."

"We have you going left of center," Eddie said. "You willing to take a breathalyzer?"

"Nah, I've been drunk. I don't need-need to walk an invisible chin, do I?"

"Nose," Carl said. "Nevermind."

"I'm gonna impound your truck and take you to the station for DUI. Understood?"

"Uh-huh."

"Put your hands behind your back," Carl said.

"I'll call for a mule," Eddie said.

They took Tyson to the station, filled out the paperwork, and with Carl behind the wheel, hit the road once again for the remainder of their shift.

Eddie thought about the question Carl asked him. About marriage. It was never on his mind. That's just the way it was. And even though Carl was married, he sensed loneliness in him. Whether he was married or not, Carl didn't have the support or the love to keep him company. Maybe long ago, but now it appeared he was on his own.

Right then, Eddie felt bad for him as well as himself, because he was on his own too. Every night he went home to no one.

He and Carl had more in common than he thought.

CHAPTER FOUR

"Sorry if I barged in on ya." Benjamin's dad took a measured seat on the couch, staring at framed newspaper articles on the far wall. "I tried callin' but got nothin' but your voice box. Figured I'd make a trip down here." He pulled out a handkerchief from the breast pocket on his overalls, blew his pitted nose, and returned it to its place.

"It's all right, Dad."

With perked ears and his tail whipping back and forth, Hogarth stood at the front door with his head lowered as if expecting someone or something.

Aisha entered the house carrying a plastic bag that had red Chinese symbols on it. She passed by Hogarth to Benjamin, who sat at his desk, and said, "Food's here." She turned to see Benjamin's dad sitting on the couch. "Hello, Mr. Cole. I thought that was your truck out there."

"Hello." He hiked up one of his pant legs to stand.

"Here," she handed the bags to Benjamin, "let me help you."

Benjamin's dad waved his leathery hand. "You sit yourself down, pretty lady. Don't want your food to get cold on you. I can handle myself just fine."

"Are you sure?"

"As sure as this eighty-three-year-old body can be." He winked at Aisha and eased his way out of the room. Hogarth followed.

Aisha turned on Benjamin. "What's wrong with you?"

"What?"

"You could've helped him up."

"He doesn't need my help. The old man is as strong as an ox." Benjamin leaned forward in his chair. "All those years living up on the farm in Bradford and you think he's not capable? Besides, he wouldn't even take your help in standing up. You really think he wants my help?"

"He's eighty-three, Ben. He's not Superman." Aisha sat in a small blue swivel chair and leaned back. "And yeah, I think he would like your help."

"Look, I know he's not getting younger, but I know damn well he's acting like some feeble old man just so I'll move up there and take care of him and the farm. I highly doubt you wanna live on a farm, now, do you?"

"You say that as though we're living together." She held up her left hand and wiggled her ring finger.

Benjamin rolled his eyes and leaned back just as his dad entered the room with Hogarth lumbering behind.

"I hope you two ain't bickering on my account."

"Everything's fine." With the bags in his hand, Benjamin stood up from his desk. "Now, who's hungry?"

Hogarth barked.

???

While Benjamin sat in his desk chair, Aisha sat on the couch next to Benjamin's dad. Dirty plates, half-emptied drinks, and empty food containers filled the coffee table in front of the couch.

Aisha retrieved her cell from her purse and checked the time. "I really need to get going. I gotta get my things packed for tomorrow's flight."

"As always, it's nice seeing you, Aisha."

"And you too, Mr. Cole." She smiled, and then leaned over and hugged him. "You take care of yourself, okay?"

"With a hug like that, I think I'm good for another year." He took Aisha's left hand and squinted at it. "Seems to be a problem with your hand."

Aisha looked down while Benjamin stepped forward. "What's the matter, Dad?"

"There's no ring." He chuckled. "When you gonna make this girl my daughter-in-law?"

Aisha covered her mouth with her right hand, trying to hide her giggles.

Without saying a word, Benjamin shook his head and left the room. He stopped at the bottom of the staircase, still within earshot of Aisha and his dad's continued conversation.

"He's lucky to have you. He'll come around though, even if I have to bend him over my knee to knock some sense into him."

"I appreciate that, Mr.—"

"I know you're being respectful and all, but you can call me Dan, ya know."

"Sorry...Dan."

"No need to be. You go gather your things in order, and I'll see ya soon."

"You take care, and we *will* see you soon. Even if I have to drag him up there."

Benjamin hurried up the stairs and disappeared around the corner.

He was sitting on the edge of the bed when Aisha entered his bedroom.

"You okay?" Benjamin didn't reply. "Look, I'm sorry about our little brouhaha downstairs. I am. But you gotta show some love to your dad." She grabbed him by the chin and tilted it up toward her. "He loves you."

He stood. "I know."

"Now go down there and spend some time with him. He drove all the way here to see you."

"I will."

"You better. This time I really have to go get ready."

She wrapped her arms around him, and he took in a deep breath.

???

"What brings you down this way?" Benjamin asked, sitting on the couch next to his dad and patting him on the leg.

"Well, since I don't get to see you often—or a phone call—I thought I'd stop in and tell ya that the farm is all yours. Put it in my will."

"What? Why?"

"Because you're my son. My only son, and I'm not gonna leave it for the yokels in DC to steal it from beneath me when I'm six feet in."

Benjamin wiped his mouth with his hand. "I mean, I knew you'd leave it to me in the end, but I wasn't expecting to have it this soon. Why now?"

"I'm not a young chicken anymore." His dad pulled out his handkerchief again and patted his forehead with it. "And my wits...well, they come and go."

Silence floated in the room like a hot-air balloon, its basket full of regrets. "I'm sorry, Dad." Benjamin's voice cracked. "I really am."

"For what?" Dan placed the handkerchief back into his pocket. "There's no need to be sorry."

"Yeah. There is. I should be up there helping you out. I've always seen you as this strong man who would rather chop his own wood than buy it."

His dad put his hand on Benjamin's shoulder. "It's okay. Would I like to see you more often? Yeah. What father wouldn't? But you got your life here. And you have a lovely woman who loves you. You got a job. You're doing well, Ben. And I'm as happy as a six-legged frog for you."

Benjamin placed his hand on his father's and gently squeezed. "I think what scares me is that it's a reality you might not be around."

"Death," his dad pulled away, "is just the beginning."

CHAPTER FIVE

Downstairs, the house phone rang and stirred Benjamin from his sleep. The clock on his nightstand read 2:36AM. He ignored the clanging and rolled over onto his stomach. After a few moments, the persistent sound silenced. He released a large sigh and tucked his arms beneath his pillow. The phone rang again.

"Okay. I'm up." He dragged himself out of bed, and patted Hogarth's head as he slept at the end of the bed. "Apparently," he yawned, "you're tired. Not a bark or anything."

He pulled up his sweatpants and flattened his t-shirt as he dragged himself downstairs to a small table by the front door. He flipped the switch on a lamp next to the phone and answered it.

"Hel…Hello," Benjamin said, rubbing his face.

"Ben?" a voice said.

Benjamin perked a little. It wasn't the voice that grabbed his attention. It didn't sound familiar, but it had called him Ben. Not Benjamin. Everyone called him by his full name. Only his dad called him Ben.

"Dad?"

"That's what I'm calling you about," the voice said. "He's… Your dad…he's…"

"Wha? Who is this?" Benjamin said.

"It's Uncle George. Your dad… He died, Ben."

"Uncle George?" Benjamin's stomach dropped. "What?! He what?" His heart sank. "How? I just saw him the other day. He was fine. When did…How?" He knelt onto the floor.

"I-I found him— Called 911. He…" His voice was distant, far off. "He committed suicide, Ben."

"What?" Benjamin squeezed his eyes shut, fighting back the tears and the anger. All the emotions and confusion swirled within him like a tornado, tearing him apart from the inside bit by bit, turning him into debris. "I don't—I don't believe it. Are you sure?"

"I found him, Ben." A sniffle came through the phone. "I found him hanging…out in the barn. Damn fool! I think you should get up—"

Benjamin cut the conversation by slamming the receiver onto its cradle. With his hands on his head, elbows on his knees, he bawled. It came hard and fast. The tears, the hitching of his shoulders, the pain. The more he thought of his dad, the harder he cried. His uncle was mistaken. He didn't commit... He didn't die the way he said he did.

Hogarth came down the stairs and sat next to him. He didn't lick his face or slip his wet nose beneath Benjamin's hands for petting, he lay down with his head between his front paws and looked up at him.

Benjamin leaned over him and buried his face into the dog's fur.

"No!"

And continued to cry.

???

His thoughts were jumbled at best as he floored the gas pedal of his Outback and raced through the darkness. Everything was a blur. Headlights. Taillights. Everything outside of him became secondary. All he knew was that his dad...

Suicide, Ben.

All he had were the scattered memories of the man he loved but didn't show it very well. Here he was on his way to see his dad because he had to, and for all the wrong reasons. There were many times he could've made the same drive without a reason, without any excuse, except for the simple fact that he wanted to. Now, he was making the trip under circumstances he wished hadn't occurred.

With tear-filled eyes, he flexed his sweaty hands a few times on the steering wheel, easing their stiffness. The radio's clock glowed 3:45AM. His heart pounded. He pressed the gas pedal down farther and continued through the night.

CHAPTER SIX

By the time Benjamin turned onto Coal Run Road, the sun was casting a morning glow across the countryside. A farm sat beyond a large field in the distance. His childhood home. A place he hadn't been to in a long time. How long was it? A weather-worn wooden fence followed alongside the road. It leaned over in places as if too lazy to stand erect. Sections were missing and broken posts remained unattended. He slowed and turned onto a dirt driveway that snaked back to the old farmhouse.

Benjamin thought it looked the same. As best as he could remember. Green patches of color spotted the rusted tin roof. Its white paint curled, chipped. Off to the side, a faded red barn sagged a little but continued to stand. *The barn.* He stared at it. It seemed to stare back. Other than some lawn work and the wooden fence needing repaired, it appeared his dad had kept the farmstead in decent shape.

This place would be in better shape if I would've come up and helped out.

Benjamin parked behind a beater of a truck and next to an old Ford Escort and threw his Outback into park. He leaned onto the steering wheel with his forearms, staring at the house for a moment, and then glanced over at a large tree stump, and a loose, brief memory of him playing with Matchbox cars at the base of an oak tree unfolded before him. Benjamin smiled at the reverie.

He cut the engine, got out, and headed toward the front door only to pause and look over at the barn.

Across the way, it sat like a tired dog. Benjamin walked over to it and stopped in its entranceway. He couldn't remember a whole lot about it except that it was where his dad kept his truck in the winter, the tractor, and various junk. He never played in there, wasn't allowed to.

He stepped into the barn. The scent of musty hay assaulted his nose. It reminded him of petting zoos rather than autumn hay-rides. He glanced down at the far end where tools hung on pegboards above two wooden work-stations that were blotted with oil and grease stains. Next to it was a rusted coffee can filled with nails sitting on the straw-covered floor.

Through the hazy air, he could almost see his dad working at the benches. Hammer in one hand, pounding on something metal, the clanging carrying into the air.

"Why'd you have to go and do something stupid?"

Benjamin took a step closer and the image of his dad in faded blue overalls flickered before him. He couldn't see his face, but he could tell he was younger. His hair was no longer full-on gray, instead it was peppered with it.

"What I'd tell ya about coming in here? This isn't a playground, y'know. You can get hurt in here." His dad's words floated through the mustiness and fell upon his ears.

"Sorry," said a little voice that sounded as if it came from Benjamin's side.

He glanced down and saw no one.

"Go on now."

When he looked back up, his dad was gone, only the work-stations in his view.

In the center of the barn, the tractor sat statuesque. Behind it, a tractor tire leaned against a darkened corner accompanied by rakes, shovels, and a pickax. Beer cans with their tops snipped off sat on exposed two by fours that made up the interior framing of the barn. Some held screws while another was full of various keys. Benjamin pulled one out. It was spotted with rust but he could see the letters *GM* on its head with clarity. A car key. He dropped it back into the can and moved around to the backside of the tractor.

On the barn's floor, a gas can sat beneath old soup cans that were nailed to the back wall. Some had buttons. Another had pennies. And another had small, colored hairclips.

It's funny, Benjamin thought, how things get collected over the years. Stuff, really. It takes an effort to collect, it takes time to collect, but it only takes about the time to write an email to discard it.

Just above eye level, different sizes of saws hung on nails by their handles. He rested his chest against the tractor and slapped it.

"Besides you, not much worth saving in here."

He looked up at the rafters and wondered which…

Not much at all.

He wiped his eyes and headed to the house, but before he could get to the door, an old man who looked to be in his late seventies came out. Benjamin knew it was his Uncle George, because it was the only family his dad had in Bradford.

He hadn't seen his uncle in a very long time, but the old man looked good. Besides the thin patch of white hair that covered his head, he was taller and thinner than his dad and walked just fine. He appeared healthy in his Dickies work pants and light blue button-down short-sleeve shirt.

"Long time no see, Ben. How are you?"

"Shocked."

"I couldn't disagree there. The deputy and everyone came this morning. They took your dad to the hospital. He'll be kept there until the funeral."

"Is that normal? Taking him to the hospital?"

"Bradford's a small town. It's the only place suitable."

"Sorry. I just— I've never…"

"It's okay. Believe it or not, I'm shocked too. He *is* my brother." George pulled out a set of keys from his pocket that had a John Deere logo key fob. "Here's the keys to the place. I'd like to stay, but I need to let this sink in a little." He looked around. "Hope you understand."

"I do," Benjamin said. "And thanks."

"Don't hesitate to call me. I left my number on the fridge."

Moments later, Uncle George waved at him as his old Escort puttered down the long dirt drive.

At the door, Benjamin tried several of the keys, and after he inserted the third and last one, it unlocked. His heart beat in his throat. His stomach flipped like a load of clothes tumbling in a dryer. He took a deep breath and pushed inside.

The living room was dusty and disheveled. Empty chip bags lay on the floor next to a couch. Its cushions were flattened, upholstery stained and worn through in spots. A tired-looking La-Z-Boy recliner sat in the corner. A Zenith console television set sat across from the couch.

The house wasn't perfect, but the ceiling and walls looked to be in good shape. Benjamin still had the kitchen, bathroom, and the bedrooms to look over, but overall, he was pleased. He was tired from the drive, drained from the emotional ride. He was hungry too, but he decided to lie on the couch and try to take a short nap instead. While lying there, all he could see were loose memories of his dad. His stomach churned. His eyes brimmed with tears.

"Gotta call Aisha!"

Throughout the entire roller coaster ride, he had forgotten all about her. He sat up and dialed her number, his thumb hovering over the *send* button.

She needed to know. His dad liked her and she liked him. If he didn't tell her, she'd be pissed. But he didn't want to ruin her time in Arizona. Would it be better to tell her after she got back? Not to give her bad news while she was two thousand miles away? It'd be a long trip back with the news of his death.

If it were him, he'd expect to know.

He pressed *send*.

She picked up after three rings.

"Hey, honey. How's it going?" she said. "Sorry I haven't called. Been busy. How have you been? How's Hogarth?"

"Well..."

Benjamin swallowed a lump in his throat. His heart hurt as it beat in his chest. If it could break, it would fall in pieces.

"Well what?"

The words gathered at the tip of his tongue but wouldn't, refused, to come out. He didn't want them to, he was afraid to let the truth escape his mouth. If he kept it locked up, then it all wasn't happening.

"What's wrong?"

But it did happen. It was happening, and he had to let her know no matter how much it hurt him to let the words go.

"My dad, he, uh, he passed away."

Silence filled the airwaves.

"My god! How?"

He squeezed his eyes tight but the tears escaped them and slid down his cheeks anyway.

"Suicide."

Nothing in return. Then, "You're kidding me, right? He wouldn't commit... My god. I'm so sorry. I am," she said. "Where are you?"

"I'm at the farmhouse in Bradford. Hogarth's with me."

"I'm coming."

"You don't—"

"I'm going to take some time off from work. I'll be there as soon as I can."

"Okay."

"I'm sorry. He was such a gentle man."

"I'm sorry too," Benjamin said, and ended the call.

For a lot of things.

CHAPTER SEVEN

He wandered through the farmhouse as his stomach grumbled. When he got to the kitchen, it was nothing out of the ordinary: gas stove, fridge, a small table with chairs, cupboards full of mismatched dishes, silverware the same, and various bottles of medication. A country border with chickens ran along the top of the walls. The room seemed familiar, but he couldn't place any specific memory to it. In the back corner, a bed sheet hung in a doorway. Benjamin pushed it aside and found the washer and dryer. Across from them there was a door. He opened it and peered in. The basement. A dank and moldy smell smacked him in the face, and he closed it. Weary, he made his way back through the living room and paused at the bathroom, which housed a claw-footed tub, sink basin, and toilet. Dirty towels draped the shower rod. Toiletries crowded the toilet's water tank. He continued to the staircase across from the front door and stopped when he noticed a small room. He hadn't seen it when he first came into the house. He didn't remember the room being there at all. Then again, what did he remember? Not much. He entered and it was empty save for two windows. He looked at its main wall that ran parallel to the stairs. It appeared out of place. He glanced out, and then back inside. It didn't make sense. Maybe his dad wanted to add another bedroom.

Benjamin pulled himself up the stairs and entered the first bedroom. It was small. Stacks of boxes all marked with different years in black scribble sat against the wood-paneled walls. One box had the word *Topps* written on it. It wasn't until now that he remembered his father used it as storage room for his collection of baseball cards.

These will be yours someday, Ben.

"I guess they are."

He moved to the next room. A '79 Pirates pennant hung on the far wall. A twin bed beneath it wore its *Star Wars* sheets—with curtains to match. Benjamin didn't enter. He fought back a barrage of tears. This was something he never expected. His bedroom had been left untouched since the day he went off to college. Had he known...

All the years I could've visited...

His shoulders slumped with regret.

...*and didn't.*

Daylight eased through a bare window and lit his father's bedroom in a gray haze. Tears dripped down his cheek. It too was small. Empty cola cups from various fast-food chains along with small pieces of yellowed paper littered the ragged carpet. A slumped king-sized bed covered with crumpled, stained sheets was pressed against the wall. It looked as if his dad hadn't used the room in a long time. He wondered how long his dad had actually been sleeping down on the couch. Had it been a few months? Years? By the looks of his nearly vacant room, it'd been quite some time. He cleared his eyes with the palms of his hands, then wiped his nose with the back of his shirt sleeve.

"All the damn years I could've visited...wasted...and on what?"

???

Hungry, Benjamin checked the fridge and found condiments past their expiration dates, an empty carton of milk, and some Tupperware with what appeared to be leftovers of some kind. Each one moldy. He shut the door and leaned against it. He didn't bother to check the freezer. He had a suspicion it wouldn't be any better. He rubbed his face. "Shit." And then slapped the fridge with his hand.

The refrigerator's empty contents were like a punch in the gut, painful.

He placed a palm on the old appliance, his arm outward, and leaned against it. "Goddamn it. Should've called me. How long?" He paused at the sob that caught in his throat. "How long did you go without, Dad? Huh? Days? Weeks?"

His dad never came to him for help. It was his way. The reality of the situation hurt more than anything.

He punched the refrigerator. A jolt of pain burst into his knuckles. "Son of a..." He shook his hand as he left the kitchen, not caring about the small dent he made in the freezer door.

On the couch he leaned back and flexed his sore hand, wincing as he did so. *I'm such a jerk.* From his dad's bedroom to the near-empty refrigerator, the house revealed things Benjamin wished he didn't know. *A damn lousy son.* For now, he had to tuck his feelings away and push forward. Had to think about the next steps. Bills. Papers to fill out. A house in need of attention. A funeral to prepare. He was tired. His head ached, his stomach ached, his heart ached, and his hand ached. Benjamin needed a good night's sleep. He loosened his Chuck Taylors, kicked them off onto the matted carpet, and lay back. He pulled the afghan from the back of the couch down on top of himself and tucked his good, and not-so-sore hand, beneath his head. The blanket smelled like a concoction of hard work and dirt. Benjamin wondered how often his dad took a shower. Maybe once a week. Maybe. The last thought that floated in his mind before darkness overcame him was the empty refrigerator.

???

Forever and ever.

Benjamin swiped at his ear and turned his head with a groan.

It's our secret!

Another swipe.

Secret.

He bolted upright. Benjamin wasn't sure if he actually heard someone's voice or if it was a dream. The television was off.

Secret.

There it was again. An older man's voice.

Was it a ghost?

CHAPTER EIGHT

The funeral was short and quick. Benjamin remained at the grave with his hands folded before him. No one besides him, Aisha, and Uncle George attended. It didn't matter whether hundreds came or not because it was family that counted. He'd hate to admit it, but Aisha's argument for marriage may have become more important now even though he still wasn't in favor of it.

Uncle George stepped up next to him. "How ya holding up?"

"Good, I guess. Under the circumstances."

Y'know? For being a terrible son?

Silence passed between them for a moment.

"What are you going to do with the farm?" said George. "It's gonna cost a fortune to keep it. Fixing it up and all."

"Don't know. Not sure if I want to sell it. It'd be like I was selling *him*."

"Well. That farmhouse *is* in need of serious repairs. It's been neglected for some time due to your father's age. Just couldn't work like he used to. It'll cost a lot to get it in shape." He placed his hand on Benjamin's shoulder. "Probably not the best time to say this, but I could take it off your hands if you want."

"I'll...uh, keep that in mind."

"I'm here if you need me."

Without looking over at his uncle, Benjamin said, "How about you come over tomorrow morning for breakfast? Give me a history lesson on the farm."

George chuckled. "Sure."

???

At the kitchen table, Aisha and George ate eggs and bacon while Benjamin washed dishes.

"You were right," Benjamin said. "There is a lot to be done here."

"No reason to lie."

"Hate to eat and run, but I gotta get back home and pick up Darren." Aisha slipped her plate and fork into the sink. "You going to be okay?"

Benjamin dried his hands. "I'll be fine."

She kissed him on the cheek and said, "I'll call you later."

"Okay."

"Love you."

"Don't speed," Benjamin said. "Love you too."

George stood. "Don't be a stranger now."

"I won't." Aisha gave him a light hug. "Thanks for coming over."

"He's family...and so are you. Don't forget, I lost a brother, and this old man needs you guys too."

Aisha hugged him again and left the room.

George patted Benjamin on the back. "Ready for that history lesson?"

Benjamin stepped out into the sun-filled morning and took in a deep breath. He scanned the grounds before him and took in the barn and the field that flanked the house with its dilapidated fence.

"Sixty-five acres in all. You probably didn't know that, did you?" said George from behind.

"Actually, no. I don't remember a whole lot about this place. Bits and pieces. It's like I never lived here. No youth. No teen years. Nothing. And I was here till I graduated from Bradford High." Benjamin pointed to a large tree. "Except for that tree. I remember playing with my Matchbox cars there. Out of everything, that's what I freakin' remember. Matchbox cars."

"I'm no doctor, but maybe you should see a therapist."

"You know what's worse? I barely remember you," Benjamin said. "How shitty is that?"

"Don't worry. It'll come. Been a long time and with your dad passing... And I'm here now. That's all that matters. The now."

Benjamin smiled. "I'm glad you're here."

"Me too."

"Well, now," Benjamin said, "what else can you tell me?"

"Let me see."

The field beyond the fence looked like a ratty quilt made by harsh weather and time. No longer lush and green. Alive. Now, as Benjamin looked on, it looked like death.

"Your dad and I used to hunt deer out here," said George with a nod of his head. "Skinned them right back there in the barn." He glanced over at Benjamin. "Probably don't remember, huh?"

"I would *definitely* remember that. But no, I don't."

George turned around and pointed toward the thick woods beyond the farmhouse.

"There's a pond out in those woods where your dad would catch snapping turtles for soup."

"I definitely don't recall that." Benjamin made a sour face. "Turtle soup?"

"Well, you were a wee one then." He chuckled. "One time we were back there fishing for bass and there were some Canada geese in the water. I don't remember what you did, but for some reason one of those crazy geese chased you around, its wings spread out and flapping, and it bit you in the back. Your dad chased it off and held you as you cried and cried." George chuckled again, louder.

"Wow. Don't remember that either," Benjamin said. "Then again, I haven't been around any geese in a long time. Subconscious fear, maybe?"

"Well, if you end up keeping this place, then maybe those memories will come back to you."

"Hope so."

Benjamin paused at the barn. Its once bright red paint now lay faded and chipped. Just as everything else on this farm, it seemed, it, too, was dead. Its large doors were open and inside he could see the tractor.

"He never let you in there. Was always afraid you'd get hurt. All those rusty nails and tools and such." He rubbed his hair back. "Getting a bit warm out here. If you don't mind, I'm gonna get home and cool off with a cold one before it gets too hot out. I'll be back later."

"That's not necessary. You've done more than needed. Thanks. I really appreciate it."

"Well, if you need me," George walked toward his car, "don't hesitate to call."

"If I remember, I will." Benjamin smiled, but the joke was lost on his uncle.

He watched his uncle's old car rumble down the dirt drive. A part of him wasn't joking about the remembering. He hadn't remembered a lot of things here. Some things he did, and he wondered why he couldn't remember everything as he headed back inside the house. He shrugged it off and gave thought to the old place. Could he fix it up? Could he keep his dad's hard work intact, alive? Keep the few memories of him alive?

CHAPTER NINE

He didn't believe in ghosts, but Benjamin wondered if his dad was watching him as he lay on the sofa in the darkened living room. He thought about the stories Uncle George told him. The image of deer carcasses hanging in the barn. Turtle soup. And a pissed off Canada goose chasing him as a young boy. He didn't remember them, but it didn't matter, because he didn't want to remember them.

He wanted to remember his dad.

The old house creaked as if it stretched its wooden bones. It seemed to have a life of its own. The stairs creaked after each step. Floorboards moaned beneath footfalls. And even though his house back in Oakmont never breathed or spoke as the farmhouse did, that wasn't what bothered him.

It was the silence.

He wasn't used to staying somewhere so quiet. At his house he could hear the Allegheny River sloshing about just steps away, sirens bellowing in the night, and neighborhood dogs barking in backyards.

A breeze fluttered the living room curtains. The cool air touched his face.

"Tell Mom I send my love," he whispered.

Once the last word fell from his mouth, he realized he never thought about his mom. His only image of her was from what he could gather from his dad's memory. Hazel eyes. Brunette hair. A beautiful woman with a sense of humor the size of Bradford itself. What his dad called a "real country girl." There were no pictures of her in the house. Only of him and his dad. And even those were rare.

"Not sure what I can do with this place, but I'll do what I can. I hope you won't be angry if I have to sell it."

The wind kicked up the curtains again as if to respond.

Before too long, Benjamin fell asleep.

He stood outside the barn.

Over his shoulder, the sun shone like a drop of honey as it settled for the oncoming of darkness. Dust and particles from the hay floated about in the dying sunlight.

Drip. Drip. Drip.

Blood pooled onto the barn floor. The sound of it splattering against the wet straw of hay turned his stomach. It was dark, almost black. He followed the continuous dripping upward and there—hanging by its neck from a rafter—was a young deer. It looked to be a doe. Small. Its skin was peeled back from its belly. Guts dangled from its cavity. Its neck painted crimson. Its fur matted. Benjamin glanced at its face. Its eyes bulged and its tongue hung loosely from its mouth.

"Don't come in here!" a voice gargled.

Benjamin couldn't see who spoke in the darkening barn. The deer hung in his way. He wasn't sure if it was his dad because it didn't sound like him. It sounded like someone or something else. He took a step back.

"How many times have I told you?"

A thin stream of blood worked its way from the puddle to Benjamin's feet just outside the barn doors.

Drip. Drip. Drip.

He couldn't help but look up at the dead deer.

In an instant, the deer bucked its bound legs, its eyes wild. It opened its mouth and screeched, "Don't come in here looking for trouble! Get out!" Blood spurted from it as it spoke. Its throat sounded as if it were filled with water, its words gurgling in Benjamin's ears.

He screamed.

Benjamin awoke to the sound of his own voice.

"Jesus!"

His heart beat through his wet chest as he wiped his hands across his face.

Aisha rushed into the living room from the kitchen. "You okay?" Hogarth trotted in right behind her. "You were screaming. You're covered in sweat."

He startled. "Geez. Give me a heart attack, why don't you."

"I'm sorry."

She sat down next to him as Hogarth nudged his head underneath Benjamin's hand.

"It's okay, I'm fine." He sat up. "Just a strange dream."

"Care to tell me?"

He rubbed Hogarth behind the ears.

"Not unless you like skinned deer talking."

"Gross."

"Thought so," Benjamin said. "I didn't hear you come in last night. Aren't you tired? All that travelling back and forth?"

"Came in early this morning. And no, I'm not tired. I wanna be here with you. What kind of girlfriend would I be if I didn't support you during this time? You'd do the same for me. Right?"

"Of course. And thank you." He grabbed her leg and gave it a gentle squeeze.

"You're welcome." She returned the gesture by squeezing his hand. "Okay, breakfast is almost ready." She stood. "Can you take Hogarth out?"

"Where's Darren?"

Aisha went into the kitchen.

"Upstairs in your bed," she hollered.

There were times Benjamin wished Aisha didn't have Darren as much as she did. Sometimes he wanted Aisha to himself. No kid. No dog. Just him and her. Not that he'd ever ask her to trade Darren in for some free time, but the alone time would be nice.

"Ah," Benjamin said.

While the big dog did his business, Benjamin thought about what his uncle had told him. He stood in the entranceway to the barn. The John Deere tractor was large. Not one of those little grass cutters you'd find back in someone's shed. A bonafide country tractor. One used to pull, drill—if the right attachment was used—dig, and the like. The tractor *was* his dad. His hard work ethic, his blue-collar blood. And that thought alone brought Benjamin to wipe his eyes clear of tears. His dad's passing was harder on him than he thought. Everything was a symbol of the man. Everything was a symbol of his regret.

"Our secret!"

He spun around. Only the heat of the day greeted him. He turned back and craned his neck toward the back of the barn. He took a step forward. No one. He was positive he heard *the* voice. He paused and remembered the first night when he slept on the couch. The voice. It was the same voice in his dream. Was it a dream? He furrowed his brows and cocked his head to the side and listened. Silence. He relaxed and went to the house.

He opened the screen door and—

"SECRET!"

This time it was clear. Someone spoke. No dreaming. It was real. Benjamin realized right then and there that he had a bigger problem than the current pile on his plate.

CHAPTER TEN

Cleveland, Ohio. July 4, 1967.

The sound of Lake Erie's waves ebbed and flowed upon the beach as the smell of suntan lotion emanated from the hundreds of people that packed the sandy shore, wearing shorts and bathing suits. Beach towels splayed out like patchwork. Laughter carried throughout the purple-bruised sky as children ran about with fizzing sparklers.

The parking lot sat far back from the soon-to-be revelers, and on a night where fireworks would blaze in the sky, it could be the best place to watch them. But it was summer, and the beach was the place to be.

Up ahead, Mindy's two teenage boys ran past her husband in between an old Safari wagon and a white Imperial LeBaron, and headed toward the beach. He turned back and waved for her. "C'mon."Beach towels were tucked beneath her arm while she carried their little girl in the other.

"I'm coming," she hollered. "Keep your eye on the boys."

"Hurry up," he yelled.

As she came between the wagon and the LeBaron, a hand reached out of the wagon and adjusted its side mirror.

Startled, she released a yelp and dropped her towels. Her little girl clung to her.

"I apologize, miss," said a man's voice from within the wagon. "I didn't mean to scare you."

"That's okay. I was hurrying to catch up with my husband. Not paying much attention."

The lamppost above blackened. The entire parking lot faded to black.

"Now how am I going to find Ron and the boys?"

"I'll turn on my headlights. That should help." The driver's side door opened. "Now let me help you with your belongings."

"Thank you. I can't put her down or she'll burst out crying."

"That's fine." He picked up the beach towels and tossed them onto the driver's seat. "She's a cutie." He took one and folded it.

"Thank you," she said."You don't have to do that."

"It's the least I can do for scaring you." He set the towel on top of the car and grabbed another from the seat. "There is an old saying my father told me as a young child." He folded it and set it on top of the other and then turned and faced her. "The devil is in the details."

With his back to the light from his headlights, she couldn't make out his face. It was still too dark.

"That's funny, I've heard it as God is in the details."

The man chuckled.

A pop came from Lake Erie, followed by a loud thundering boom. Red streaks of light streamed outward. Seconds later, a yellow flower bloomed in the night sky.

"Look, Marie." She pointed out above the lake. Greens and purples reflected off the water's surface, mirroring it's beautiful but dangerous displays of colors. "Pretty fireworks." An explosion filled the air with an echoing din that carried out in all directions. It startled her. "That was a loud one." Without looking back at the man, she said, "I better go and find my husband and boys. They're probably wondering where I'm at."

"Don't let me hold you up. I am sure they are worried." The man grabbed the two folded towels from atop his wagon and handed them to her. While she tucked them beneath her arm, he reached in and cut the headlights. "Fireworks are best in total darkness."

The little girl sat in her mother's arm and gazed at the fiery display, unfazed by the din of the cheering people.

"We should be going. Thank you for folding my towels. That was kind of you."

"You are welcome. Enjoy the fireworks."

A quick succession of red flowers sprouted in the night garden, grabbing her attention. Thin streams blasted outward in all directions. Yellows, purples, and whites followed. The revelers ooohed and aaahed, their voices rolling into the parking lot like a wave. The pungent odor of spent fireworks filled the air.

With her daughter in one arm and the towels in her other, pain exploded from her abdomen. And it took her breath away. She looked down. The man had a push blade jammed into her gut. He pulled it out, and then in a swift motion cut across her stomach. She released a groan and stumbled back. Against the white Imperial, her legs gave and she slid down onto her rear, her daughter clutched in her arms. A loud pop came from Lake Erie, and then above her, a snap released a fiery rose. The crowd's reaction drowned out her little girl's cry.

Rapid bursts of whites, reds, yellows, and greens pierced the sky and illuminated it intermittently like a giant strobe light. The man grabbed her daughter from her arms.

Darkness.

The sky flashed bright with numerous white bursts.

Her little girl's face exploded with tears. Mindy tried to scream, but the pain was too much. The sensation of fire seared into her stomach. Her breath hitched.

Darkness.

Consecutive crimson blossoms bathed the scene of the man putting the little girl into the front seat of his wagon.

Darkness.

Mindy closed her eyes.

Darkness.

She opened them to see green and gold occupy the night. The silhouette of the man swayed as if she were on rough seas. He faded, then came into view. He stood over her and wiped his blade on one of her towels.

She reached up toward him. Her hand covered in blood.

"The Devil's *always* in the details," he said.

He faded.

Her little girl's cry faded.

She dropped her hand.

Darkness.

CHAPTER ELEVEN

"This is fun, huh?" Aisha said. "We haven't had a day like this in a while. Just us three hanging out."

"And eating ice cream," Darren said, taking another lick.

Hogarth waited on his haunches with wet jowls.

They sat at a park bench next to a small ice cream stand where several townspeople waited in line to order. She couldn't help but notice a young woman holding a baby girl. Aisha smiled and looked at Darren, and then back to the baby. She wanted another child. A sister or brother for Darren. She didn't want him to be an only child, alone. Aisha knew that feeling as she grew up. The loneliness. And she didn't want that for her son. If only Benjamin felt the same about kids. He didn't want any. She could understand that, but what she couldn't understand was why not marry her? They'd had their arguments over the subject, but he never gave her a clear reason. She needed to know why.

"This is good," Darren said, snapping her away from her thoughts.

"Huh? Yeah, I bet. I gotta take a mental photo of this. Stow it away for when you're older, out of the house."

"I'm never leaving the house. It's where my toys are. And Hoagie."

She smiled. "I hope you never leave. Don't ever grow up."

Among the customers in line for ice cream, a young man with dirty-blond hair stared at her, and when he realized she saw him, he looked away. Aisha had the feeling she'd seen him before. But where? He glanced back at her, stepped out of line, and walked away with a baseball cap in his hand.

"Wish Benjamin would've come for ice cream," Darren said.

She watched him cross the street. He glanced back at her as he turned onto another street. A group of teenagers passed him, obscuring her view, and when they dispersed to the ice cream stand, he was gone.

"Mommy?"

"Huh?"

"Don't you wish Benjamin was here?"

"Yeah, I do, but he's taking care of things at the farm. He's got a lot on his mind." She rubbed his head and forced a smile. "I'm sure he'd rather be here eating ice cream with us. Ready? Wanna explore some more?"

"Yeah." He gave Hogarth the remainder of his vanilla cone.

After they wiped their hands and mouths clean, she tossed napkins into a garbage can, and they walked down the sidewalk.

"So is the Udder Shack a keeper?" she said.

"Yep," Darren said. "It's a keeper."

Hogarth paused at a small tree and raised his leg, claiming it. Aisha tugged his leash as he sniffed at its base, and they continued walking along the shaded sidewalk, which gave temporary shelter from the sun. After a few blocks of passing locals who replied with "hellos" and "that dog should be wearing a saddle," which always got a laugh from Darren, they made their way onto another tree-lined street for no reason other than to keep walking without direction.

The houses sat farther apart from one another than the homes in town, and sat farther back from the road as well. Long gravel driveways cut paths to their respective garages. The houses weren't special or larger than the others; they were normal and nothing more. The street ended in a cul-de-sac, and they stopped to rest in the shade on someone's front lawn. Aisha sat with one arm around Darren while the other wiped her sweaty forehead.

"Hot, huh?"

"Yeah," Darren said.

Hogarth's tongue slapped from side to side at his mouth, and he lay down.

"Good idea," Aisha said. "Let's all rest for a while and then head back to the car. The air conditioning will do us some good." She lay back onto the grass and pulled Darren with her. With knees bent and Darren's head on her chest, she closed her eyes.

She faded into sleep only to be awoken by Hogarth, whose tags clanked against one another. He released a small bark just beneath his breath. Aisha opened her eyes. "What are you yapping about?" He stared at the house across the road. Ears perked. Darren sat up next to him. Another whispered bark.

She sat up.

White sheer curtains fell back into place in the large bay window.

"What'd you see, boy?" she said.

Hogarth looked at Darren, and then back, and then gave him a quick lick on the face.

"Aw, Hoagie." Darren wiped his face with his palm. "Right in the nose."

"C'mon," Aisha said, "let's go."

As they headed back, Aisha felt somewhat refreshed from the quick power nap, but she had a strange feeling that didn't sit well with her. Like…Anxiety crept into her chest and caused her heart to flitter for a moment like a hummingbird zipping back and forth. Like… She peered back over her shoulder at the house.

Like someone watched them.

CHAPTER TWELVE

Evening had settled. At the kitchen table, Aisha ate corn on the cob and pork chops. Darren's plate was half-empty. He took a gulp of his milk, then wiped his mouth with the back of his hand.

"That's what your napkin is for, sweetie. Use it next time, okay?"

Benjamin sat down to where his plate had already been made, glass of milk next to it. He looked over at Darren, and then at Aisha.

"Can I go play? I'm full."

"Sure. Go ahead," Aisha said.

Darren took another drink of his milk, used his napkin to clean his mouth, and ran off into another room.

"Have a good nap?" she said.

"Had better." Benjamin grabbed the salt and dashed it on his corn on the cob. He set the shaker down, picked up his corn, and took a bite. "Good stuff, huh?"

She didn't reply. She only rubbed her ring finger as she chewed her food.

He knew what was coming. He was surprised it took this long to rear its head. Usually, it showed up once a week. He figured his dad's passing gave him a break from it. The break was over.

"Can I ask you something without you getting mad?" she said. "Without an argument?"

"Think I'm gonna go down to the cemetery," Benjamin said.

Before he could get up, Aisha said, "Cemeteries close at dusk." She glanced out the kitchen window. "It's dark out. And running from this won't help, y'know."

"What are you talking about?"

"Marriage. Why won't you propose to me? We've been together for two years, a little longer, actually. You know I want to get married, but *you* don't. Is it because you don't want kids?"

"What?!" He got up. "Is this because I didn't go get ice cream with you?"

"You get along with Darren—for what it's worth—so I don't see what the problem is. I'm confused. When we *do* talk about it, you say you love me." In a quick motion, she scooted her chair back, its legs scraping across the floor."If you do, then why can't you marry me? Simple question."

"I *do* love you. I just don't want to get married."

"Why? Tell me exactly why. You know I want another baby. What is it about children that you won't marry me?"

"I don't know. Maybe it's some subconscious thing. I don't know. I mean…sometimes I do wonder…I'm confused too, y'know."

"Wonder what?" She got up and stood before him.

"If it'd be easier if we separated for a while," he said. "Just because of all the arguing over marriage."

"*Easier?* You never told me this is how you feel."Aisha's face told Benjamin everything. Her eyes were filled with tears. Brows furrowed. Nostrils flared. Anger carved into it.

"I didn't mean to hur—"

"You don't want to marry me. No problem. You got your wish. And with a bullshit of an answer."

Benjamin didn't reply. He had no words to come back with.

"So you've been stringing me along all this time? And when you felt it would be best to be on your own, you'd what? Just up and end this?" She stood in his face and wiped her tears away. "Guess I was the fool for loving you."

Benjamin's ego stepped in and put the final nail into the proverbial coffin.

"Being alone now would be good."

Aisha's face scrunched, and more tears flowed.

"I hope you think about what you've just said. And did. And here I thought you were a better man than Tyson. Guess I was wrong. You're an asshole!"

She stormed from the room and yelled for Darren to gather his things. Before Benjamin knew it, Aisha, Darren, and Hogarth were in her car and on their way back to Pittsburgh.

Benjamin sat and finished his cold meal with loneliness keeping him company.

CHAPTER THIRTEEN

They'd their share of arguments over the last two years. No doubt about it. Their fights were fast and short for the most part. She knew she rode him about marriage. Making comments here and there about it, and she meant them, but she also made them as a kind of joke that he never took as such. Rather than sitting down and having a real conversation about the subject, a conversation that wouldn't lead to a fight, it sat there on the shelf only to be brought down when needed. It never gathered dust.

But the callousness of his words hit her harder than usual this time. He didn't need to be an asshole. Maybe he didn't give a shit anymore. Maybe she didn't give a shit anymore.

But she did, and she choked back a sob. She hoped he did too.

"Mommy?" Darren said from the back seat.

"Yeah, sweetie?"

"Why are you crying?"

She wiped her eyes with her hand.

"Just sad is all. Nothing to worry about," she said. "How's Hogarth doing?"

"He's asleep. I think we need a bigger car. He's scrunched up on the seat."

"I'm sure he is. And yeah, we need a bigger car. A family car."

She reached into her purse, pulled out a tissue, and dabbed her eyes.

Family. With Benjamin, she felt as if they were a family. Overall, he was a good guy. Funny. Serious. Caring. *Did he care? Didn't show it to his dad that much. So...*

After her years with Tyson, it was great being with Benjamin. It was right being with him. At least, it felt right. And she was sure it was right.

As sure as the day she met him.

She and Benjamin had shared the same friend, Carol Woodruff, who taught Literature at the University of Pittsburgh. Carol wore a pantsuit and had her long, graying hair pulled back with a clip. She and Aisha sat outside of the University's Cathedral of Learning eating lunch in the sun-filled day.

"How's Carnegie Mellon treating you these days?" She took a bite of her egg salad sandwich.

"Good," Aisha said. She lowered her shades from her head and placed them over her eyes. "Can't complain. I really like it there."

"That's half the battle, isn't it? Finding a job that you like. Or one that can become a career that you love. Like mine. I'm happy where I am with Pitt."

Aisha took a sip from her water bottle.

"So what's the other half of the battle?"

"Huh?"

"You said that having a job you like is half the battle. What's the other half?"

"Oh." Carol laughed. "Family and good friends."

"That's more than half, don't you think?" Aisha said.

"Then it's not half, it's two-thirds? Career. Family. Friends. Get all those right, then you've got happiness. Worked for me."

"Well, I've got a career I love. Got Darren. All my old friends are no longer good friends. We've kind of separated as the years passed."

"What about coworkers?"

"I've got some friends there, but we don't hang out. Just work together."

"You got me," said Carol.

"I do, don't I?"

"Carol?" a voice called out.

A tall man wearing glasses, jeans, and a button-down shirt and tie came over. Carol set her sandwich and brown paper bag down and stood.

"Benjamin. How are you?"

The two gave one another a friendly hug.

"Fine. Have today off so I'm heading to the library. You?"

"I'm fin—"

Aisha cleared her throat.

"Oh, Benjamin, this is Aisha. Aisha, Benjamin."

Aisha stood and fixed her long skirt and blouse.

"Hi," she said, and smiled.

"Hello." He smiled back, adjusting his glasses.

"Benjamin here is single," Carol said, "and a journalism professor at Point Park."

"You are?" Aisha said.

"Yeah. Been teaching for quite some time."

"No, I meant being single."

She giggled at the memory. Aisha had been pretty forward back then. Still was, but now it pushed Benjamin away. Before, her confidence was a characteristic he loved. Thinking back to that day, Aisha knew that Benjamin wasn't the same person that made her come on to him so quickly. Now, he was… She didn't know, really. *Unhappy?* Was that it?

Aisha wanted a stable relationship, a family. A solid family life to raise Darren in. And she needed the support as well. She loved Benjamin, and she knew he loved her, but…

She laid her head back against the headrest.

Maybe I should turn right around and go fight for my family. Straight up. No more bullshit.

Maybe…maybe she should end it. Concentrate on herself and Darren. Let things, or life, happen rather than force it. Was that it? She was too forceful? About everything? Not just marriage or to Benjamin, but about every choice she made or considered.

No. She always knew what she wanted. Whether it was her career at Carnegie Mellon or Benjamin. She liked CMU, and after graduation she stayed and worked for the institution that was her alma mater. She liked Benjamin too, and she went after him.

Marriage, however…

It's not forcefulness; it's determination and persistence.

If she left him, it would be a hard decision.

I can't ignore it. I have to consider it.

Aisha would have to leave marriage on the shelf for a while. It'd get dusty. Would need a cleaning every now and then, but right now she'd take a day or two back at home to get her head straight, and then get to the bottom of the whole relationship and where it stood for the both of them.

CHAPTER FOURTEEN

The headstone was simple. It had the obvious information written on its face. Name. Birth date. Date of passing. And the small inscription: *A Beloved Father, Brother, and Friend.*

Benjamin stood before the marker. He didn't know what to say and felt a little silly for coming. Would his dad hear him? Or would he be speaking to an expensive piece of stone? He came for a reason, and so he tried his best to not feel a little crazy for speaking to no one in particular.

"You probably know that Aisha and I are kaput. Not that you're watching us. I'm sure you're with mom, rekindling old times." Benjamin paused for a moment. "You're not watching us, are you?"

In the distance, a man and a woman stood at a large tombstone. *Brother and sister, maybe. A couple.* The man wrapped his arm around the woman's shoulder and pulled her in and leaned his cheek on top of her long, curly hair. Benjamin turned back to his dad's small gravestone.

"I've done a lot of stupid crap, haven't I? You deserved a better son. I never visited you." His eyes welled. "I live no more than four and a half hours away and I never made the effort to come up here and see you. Never! You always came to me. And that wasn't right, Dad. I *should* have come to you." He wiped his eyes and nose with his arm. "Aisha was right. I'm an asshole. She was supportive and loving, and what did I give in return? Nothing. No love. Definitely no marriage."

He released a loud sigh and glanced back over at the couple. They were gone. He turned to his dad and said, "You know why I haven't married her? Because there's this weird part of me that doesn't want to have kids. And she wonders why I'm not overly excited about Darren. I mean, he's a good kid, don't get me wrong, but I just can't. If I marry her, I *know* we'll have a kid. I know it."

Silence.

"I can't be a father. I can't be what you were. And I have no clue as to why I feel like this. None! I'm just screwed up, I guess." Benjamin knelt onto the grass, sniffled, and said, "I don't know if I can be one. And in the process, I've lost Aisha. I need her, Dad."

After he composed himself, Benjamin reached over and touched his dad's marker. "If you were here, I'm sure you'd be saying some crazy line." He cleared his throat and in his best Dad voice said, "Son, you can't squeeze blood from a stone. And if you can, then try a piece of coal in your rear, cuz you've got something you can't ever lose, too valuable to give up."

He stood and wiped his knees free of grass.

"Never really could understand your point whenever I did hear one...but...I messed up and I need to get my diamond back, or blood, whatever that means."

He looked about the cemetery. His only companions, a field full of graves, and his dad.

"Thanks for the ears."

He walked away feeling better about his situation. Whether his dad was there to listen didn't matter, because as long as Benjamin felt he did, it made all seem right.

"I gotta fix this."

CHAPTER FIFTEEN

It seemed like forever since Benjamin had been back home. He figured his mail and newspapers were piling up, and the neighbors might get worried and think he was kidnapped.

The house can wait.

"Gotta call Aisha first." With one hand, he dialed her cell, and when he got her voice-mail, he muttered, "Damn it." A beep came at his ear. "Aisha, we need to talk. Okay? I'm on my way now. Please call me back when you get this. I'm sorry. I am. Love you."

He ended his call, setting his cell into the center console, and turned on the radio, but decided against it and turned it off. Instead, he would enjoy the silence and scenery.

The drive through the wilderness and open farmland reminded him of why he left Bradford in the first place. At eighteen he would go and explore the world. To leave the small town he was raised in and see what existed outside of it. Unbeknownst to him, he would travel no farther than Pittsburgh, a mere four and a half hours away. Unbeknownst to him, it would take the death of his dad for him to return home.

His thoughts turned to Aisha, and he wondered if she would take him back. They had conquered past arguments, but yesterday's was the worst, and she was angry—really angry. He was sure she'd take him back. She always did, but he still felt nervous about it. Scared. He hoped she would take him back. Prayed she would take him back. But it was out of his control. He said what he said, and that was that.

For the first time, Benjamin thought about marriage. He ran scenarios through his head. He knew, from past quarrels, she wanted to run to Las Vegas and get hitched in the Little White Chapel. Or motor up to Camden, Maine, where they could overlook the sea from Mt. Battie.

But if he were to marry her, he felt he needed to do it right—a church with family and friends. Benjamin loved her, and now he chided himself for not making her happy, by not taking the leap. He needed to set things right.

The reverie made him feel happy, giddy, as if a kaleidoscope of butterflies were let loose inside his stomach. With a glance in the mirror, he saw a smile on his face.

"Got to do it. Time to—"

Up ahead, something big bounded out of the woods, causing him to slam his foot down on the brakes. His car skidded to the side of the two-lane road where it stopped in a patch of grass. His heart pounded against his chest. He took in a few deep breaths. His hands ached as they gripped the steering wheel, knuckles white. Standing on the broken center line of the street was a deer. It was unfazed by the near-death experience. It looked as though it was staring at him.

Don't come in here!

The image of the dead deer hanging in the barn from his dream snapped into his head. Its legs bound. Skinned and bloodied.

How many times have I told you?

Benjamin's leg tightened, reminding him that he continued to press his foot down on the brake pedal. He threw the car into park, released a deep sigh of relief, and rested his forehead against the steering wheel.

Our secret.

Startled, Benjamin spun around, looking in his back seat, and then out the passenger side window toward the woods. He turned back to the road, to the deer, but it was gone.

CHAPTER SIXTEEN

Pittsburgh, Pennsylvania. March 17, 1997.

Paul stepped onto Wood Street from the PAT bus with his little sister, Anna, and grabbed her hand. Hundreds of people all wearing green, decorated in face paint, hats, and accessories, lined the sidewalk.

"Come on, let's go see Mom," Paul said. "Don't let go."

The bus rumbled away, exhaust burning Paul's nose. He waved at the puff of black smoke that faded into the air.

Anna coughed and pulled away. "I'm not five, y'know." She covered her mouth with her hands, "I'm seven," and coughed again. "I don't need to hold your hand."

He grabbed her again and said, "Yes you do."

Paul tugged her across the street, squeezing past a group of girls, and headed up Forbes Avenue to Market Square. As they drew nearer, the number of people grew thicker, packed. He peered over his shoulder. "Hold on," he said, his outstretched hand gripping hers. He jostled against several men and women and tried to pull her through.

"Excuse me," he said.

"Hey, watch it, kid," said a woman's voice.

Before Paul could get Anna through, her hand slipped from his.

"Paul!" she cried out.

He turned and bobbed, but the sea of people blocked his view. He couldn't see his little sister.

"Anna!" he shouted and pushed past some teenage boys. "Anna!"

His heart raced.

He wanted to cry, but his adrenaline kept him in the moment.

A hand grabbed his shoulder and turned him around while arms wrapped around his waist.

"Paul!" she cried, hugging him.

A police officer stood before him. His uniform needed cleaning. It had spots of dirt on it. As if he worked on a construction site somewhere rather than the streets of downtown. The lackluster badge on his chest was in need of a shine too.

"You lose someone?" said the officer.

Paul put an arm around Anna. "Thought you were lost."

"Me too," she said.

"She said you're her brother? Is that correct?"

"Yeah. She didn't want to hold my hand and we got separated."

"Where are your parents?" said the officer.

With his arm around Anna, Paul said, "Our mom works at Primanti's. That's where we're heading."

The officer looked him over. "How old are you? Sixteen?"

"Seventeen," Paul said, a tone of offense in his voice.

"Seventeen or not. You got to be careful."

"I know."

"And how about you?" said the officer, kneeling down to Anna. "How old are you?"

"Seven."

"Seven or not, you gotta hold your brother's hand. There's a lot of people down here today, and we don't want something bad to happen to you. The city's not for a young girl like yourself."

Anna looked up at Paul, and with a sound of defeat in her voice said, "Okay, I will."

"Follow me," said the officer, standing.

As all three weaved in and out of the crowded street, Paul held onto Anna's hand as he followed the officer.

???

"Thank you, Officer," said their mother, a hint of anger in her words.

The officer turned to Paul and Anna, who sat at a small table by a long wooden counter that ran down the length of the small eatery. "You two watch yourselves, okay?"

They nodded.

The officer left, and their mom came from around the counter.

"What in the hell are you two doing here anyway? You know better than to bring her down here, Paul."

"She kept nagging me to go over to Chelsea's house and play, and I couldn't take it."

"So you brought her down here?" said his mom. "I think *you* wanted to come down here and hang out with your friends instead of babysitting your sister."

Anna giggled.

She glared at Anna. "It's not funny, missy."

Anna's head drooped, eyes downward.

With her attention back on Paul, she said, "And you could've called. That's what phones are for."

"But—"

"No buts, mister. Now, I want you to take her back home, immediately. Hear me?"

"Yes, ma'am," muttered Paul.

"You have money for the bus?"

"Yes."

"Now go. And when—"

"Excuse me," said a man with a paper bag in his hand. "Are there restrooms in here?"

"No, I'm sorry," Mom said. "There's porta-potties outside in the square, though."

The man knelt down to Anna. "Did you enjoy the parade, cutie?"

"I didn't see it."

"Missed a good one," said the man. "Maybe next year."

"Again, sorry about the restrooms," said Anna's mom.

He stood. "Thanks."

Paul watched him leave, but before he exited the restaurant, he paused at the doorway, pulled out his wallet, and began searching through it.

"Paul?" said his mother.

"Huh? Yeah."

"When I get home tonight, I'll order pizza." She put her hand on Anna's shoulder. "And Paul, I want you to hold onto your sister's hand." She looked down at Anna. "And you hold onto his. Good and tight. Got it?"

Paul's gaze fell back to the man, who put his wallet back into his back pocket, pushed through the door, and stepped out into the crowded square.

"Paul? Are you listening?"

"Yeah. Can we go now?"

"Yes, you can go."

Paul and Anna got up and she kissed them both on the cheek. "I'll see you both later."

"Love you," Paul said.

"Love you, Mom." Anna smiled.

"Love you too," she said as she returned behind the counter and helped a coworker at the register.

???

The man sat in the back of the bus and watched Paul and Anna in the front bicker with each other. He didn't care to know their argument, but assumed it had to do with their mother back at Primanti's. He dug into his brown bag, pulled out a wrapped sandwich, and began eating it. The other riders around him gave him stares.

An elderly lady leaned in and said, "Not supposed to eat on the bus, you know?"

With his mouth full, he forced a smile and turned his back to her. As he continued to eat, he kept his stare on the two kids.

???

Paul pulled the yellow cord, and the bell rang. As the bus began to slow down, he slipped money into a machine and they got off. He grabbed Anna's hand, and they trudged up a sloped street. Cars lined each side with the exception of a few metal folding chairs, which sat in empty spots, safeguarding the owner's space for their return. The houses sat above the road, cement stairways leading to their porches.

Once at the top, they turned onto a tree-lined street and walked along its sidewalk. Across the road, a dog chained to its front porch barked at them. Paul ignored it. Anna pulled her hand away.

Paul stopped. "Hold my hand."

"No. It's all wet."

She folded her arms in protest.

"Fine, I'll leave you here then."

"Fine," she said.

Paul walked onward. "Okay."

A voice yelled at the dog to be quiet. It stopped.

He glanced back at her. She remained defiant in following him, brows furrowed, arms still folded.

"Come on!" he said.

"No," she said, and turned her back to him.

He hid behind a large oak tree.

The dog barked.

Paul looked around the tree toward the road and could see the dog across the way pulling against its chain, barking. He peeped around the other side of the oak, and Anna was gone.

"Anna." He came out from his hiding spot. "Anna!" He hurried down the walk and stopped where she had stood.

From behind a maple, she jumped out and yelled, "Boo!" And laughed.

Paul flushed with heat. A mixture of anger and embarrassment.

"Not funny," he said. "Not funny at all." He grabbed her hand. "Come on."

"Ow, you're hurting me!"

He ignored her and pulled her along.

The dog across the street was reprimanded again, and silenced.

They crossed the road and continued halfway down the next block, walked through a small yard, and up to the front door of a small ranch-style house. Paul inserted a key into its lock, and seconds later, he and Anna stepped inside.

???

When a knock came at the door, Paul paused the video game at hand and answered it. A man wearing a *Kiss me, I'm Irish* t-shirt and jeans stood with a pizza box in his hand.

"Uh, I think you have the wrong address," Paul said. "I didn't order a pizza. Sorry."

"You're right, you didn't. But your mother did," said the man. "She called the shop and ordered it. Paid for it with a credit card. Thirty minutes later, here I am."

"Oh, cool," Paul said.

Anna came from another room. "Oooh, pizza."

The man stepped inside. "I'd like to set this down if you don't mind. Kinda hot."

Paul stepped back. "You can set it on the coffee table in the living room."

"I'll get the paper plates," said Anna.

Paul shut the front door and paused when he noticed the rusted old red wagon parked in front of the house.

"Is that your ride?" he said as he closed the door.

The man set the pizza down and said, "You like that rust bucket?"

"Yeah, it's sweet."

"I grabbed some napkins too," said Anna as she entered the living room.

Paul took them from her. "Pepsi?"

"You sure are bossy," she said, and returned to the kitchen.

"So what kind of car is that?"

"1955 Safari wagon. It was my dad's."

"Man, it'd be so cool to have one of those."

"Wanna ride?" said the man.

Paul was taken aback. "Uh, no thanks."

"I'm sorry. That came off wrong."

"It's okay," Paul said as he set the paper plates and napkins down on the coffee table next to the pizza box.

"I should be going." The man stepped over to the door. "Got more deliveries to make." He held out his hand.

"Oh, she didn't include a tip?" Paul searched his jeans and pulled out two crumpled dollar bills. "I have some change too." He dug back into his pocket.

"That's okay," said the man. "I gotta run."

"Two glasses of Pepsi," said Anna, walking into the living room. She sat on the couch and placed them on the coffee table and opened the pizza box.

The man smiled. "She'll be tip enough."

"What?" Paul said.

"Hey, there's no pizza in this box!"

? ? ?

Darkness settled upon another Saint Patrick's Day, and Paul and Anna's mom entered the house, looking a mess. Her hair lay in loose strands. Her sweatshirt stained. In her hand, a brown paper bag. She locked the door behind her.

"Instead of pizza I brought home some sandwiches." She placed her keys and purse onto a hook, turned around, and said, "We'll get pizza to—"

On the coffee table, a pizza box sat open, empty. Spotless. Paper plates, napkins, and cups lay scattered on the floor. The carpet looked wet.

"Paul? Anna?"

She went into the kitchen and found nothing. She ran past the bathroom and searched their bedrooms. They were empty.

"Paul!"

Where are they? It's not like them to be gone. A lump lodged in her throat. *Oh, God.*

"Anna!"

Her heart slammed against her chest.

A thump came from the bathroom, followed by a crash. She ran to it and burst into the room.

Blood splattered the walls and tiled floor. The mirror above the small sink basin was streaked red. The room smelled foul, as if meat had been left on the counter. She backed out and hit into the hallway wall, her hand trembling as she covered her mouth.

"Oh god!"

The shower rod and curtain that lay in the tub moved. A cherry-stained hand reached out.

"M-mom," Paul said. "H-help."

His mother ran to him and threw off the rod, pushed aside the curtain. There, wet with crimson, Paul lay with closed eyes. His breathing labored.

Tears tumbled from her eyes.

"Paul. My god. What…what happened?"

"I…I'm s…sorry," he stammered. "I-I…tried."

She wanted to take him out of the tub, to hug him.

"Tried what? Where's Anna?"

Without another word she ran into the living room and grabbed her purse. She emptied it onto the floor, snatched her cell phone, and called 911.

When she returned to the bathroom, she knelt next to the tub and said, "Hang on, Paul. Okay?"

He didn't respond.

"Paul?"

He no longer breathed.

"Paul!"

CHAPTER SEVENTEEN

Benjamin never received a call back from Aisha, and she wasn't at her place either. After he went home and gathered his mail and newspapers from his porch, he stopped at the Three Rivers Grill for some food. He would try Aisha again later. Happenstance was on his side, though, or possibly his dad, because when he pulled into the parking lot of the eatery and cut the engine, his cell rang.

Aisha's name appeared on the caller ID.

He flipped it open and without giving her a chance to say anything he blurted, "I'm so sorry. Please don't hate me. Okay? I love you."

After a few moments of silence, she sighed and said, "I love you too. You really pissed me off, you know? I seriously thought about ending it. Thought if you didn't want to be with me, then why bother?"

"I *do* want to be with you, and I'm willing to sit down and talk about this. I am. I care about you and Darren."

"Really?"

"Yeah, really. Look, I'm at the Three Rivers Grill." Benjamin crossed his fingers. "Come and meet me."

A few seconds of silence passed between them.

"Okay," she said. "I'm still mad, though. Doesn't mean everything is A-okay. Got it?"

"Got it." Benjamin smiled. "And rightfully so."

"I'll be there shortly," she said.

She hung up without saying her usual, "I love you." It hurt him, but he understood. He didn't fault her for it. It was his fault, and he'd have to make it up to her over time. His relationship was intact, and that's all that mattered. He hadn't lost her.

???

They sat opposite one another in the booth, Darren next to Aisha.

"I don't wanna get into things real deep with…" Benjamin eyed Darren, who was coloring on a paper placemat, "…here, y'know?"

"I know. When we have some alone time," she said.

"Yeah. And I do wanna talk about it. It's only right."

A middle-aged woman set three plates of food onto their table. "Anything else?"

"I'm fine," Benjamin said.

"Me too," Aisha said.

Darren grabbed a fry from his plate and stuck it into his mouth.

"I'll take it he's fine too," said the waitress.

"He's good," Aisha said. "Thanks."

The woman smiled and walked to another table and began taking an order.

Benjamin took a bite of his sandwich. "Who would've thought putting coleslaw and Swiss on hot roast beef would be this good?"

"Not me," Aisha said.

Benjamin held out his sandwich. "Wanna bite?"

"No thanks. I'm fine with what I have."

He wiped his chin free of slaw sauce with a napkin, took in a deep breath, and sighed.

"What?" she said.

Benjamin leaned back. "At the farmhouse. Did you…did… Have you heard anything?"

"Like what?"

"Anything that didn't seem normal? Out of place?"

"No, not that I know of."

"I hear crickets," Darren said. His chin had a smudge of ketchup on it.

Benjamin leaned in and held his hand up to his mouth to block Darren from hearing him. He whispered, "What if I told you that for a while now I've been hearing voices?"

"I can hear you," Darren said.

Benjamin joined Aisha's laughter as she slid a crayon to Darren and said, "Why don't you color while you finish your food? Not nice to listen to someone else's conversation."

"Can't help it."

"Look," she said to Benjamin. "You've been under a lot of stress with your dad's passing and the house and all. It's rough."

"And us too," he said.

"And, yeah, us too. Like I said, it's been rough. But I think it's just your imagination. From the stress." Aisha leaned forward and whispered, "I don't think you're crazy, if that's what you're thinking."

Darren continued coloring and didn't add anything to the topic.

"Well, crazy or not, I have been hearing it. I think."

"I'm sure it's nothing. Just an anxiety overload, that's all."

"Maybe you're right. Things have been stressful…for the both of us." Benjamin pulled back. "I'm *not* crazy, right?"

"If you are, then that makes the four of us."

It took a moment, but Benjamin started laughing at her silly joke and Aisha joined him.

CHAPTER EIGHTEEN

A few days later, Benjamin, Aisha, and Darren made the best out of the day's heat by having a picnic in the shade at Bradford Park.

Benjamin sat with his legs crossed on a blanket beneath a large tree and watched Aisha and Darren play on the monkey bars. With a bottle of Coke in his hand, and for what seemed a long time coming, he smiled at the two.

"This is nice."

While Darren hung from the monkey bars, Aisha gave him several raspberries on his exposed stomach. He laughed and let go of the bars, only to have her wrap him up in her arms and continue her wet assault.

Children ran about in the park. Some chased one another, others climbed up slides, and some popped up and down on the teeter-totters like prairie dogs appearing and disappearing from their holes. Most parents kept to the shade and watched from afar.

???

And so did the man who hid in the surrounding woods.

The man's face was pressed to a viewfinder of a Canon camera. He wore a long-sleeved shirt with Dickies up to his waist and green suspenders strapped over his hunched shoulders. A large-brimmed hat rested upon his head.

Through the camera he peered at two young girls of about seven sitting in the grass playing with Barbies. He pressed his forefinger.

Click!

He swiveled the telephoto lens to an older man pushing a little boy on a swing.

Another press.

Click!

The man panned the lens across the park and stopped on a little boy chasing his mother around in the grass. His chalk-like fingers turned the lens—zooming in on them and—

Click!

Another picture preserved the moment.

He packed his gear and fastened the string beneath his chin, securing his hat in place. Out in the park, the mother gave the little boy a piggyback ride toward a man sitting on a blanket with a bottle of pop in his hand. Without the camera lens, they looked a lot farther away. He shouldered his camera bag and began walking back through the woods.

???

Aisha set Darren down as they came toward Benjamin, who was nursing his Coke.

"You see me catch Mommy?"

"Yeah, I did. You're fast, buddy. Want to help me fold the blanket?"

"I don't wanna go," Darren said.

"Not even for ice cream?" Aisha said.

"Yeah," Darren said. "Ice cream!"

Benjamin and Darren provided the cheers as they pulled out of the parking lot and headed into town. "Ice cream. Ice cream."

A few blocks down, they came to a red light. Aisha busied herself by singing Beyonce's latest song while Darren sat strapped in his booster seat and kicked his legs to the beat. In the passenger seat, Benjamin ignored the din in the car and watched a man up ahead carry a tripod and a camera bag down the sidewalk. The light turned green, and they passed him. Benjamin watched him grow smaller in his side mirror and wondered why anyone would wear Dickies and a long-sleeved shirt on such a hot day.

???

Sweat stained the pits and neckline of the man's shirt while he carried his camera equipment up the gravel driveway to his ranch-style house. He pulled out a large ring of various keys and flipped through them until he came to a gold key with a blue cap. He unlocked four deadbolts and then picked out another key with a red cap. He inserted it into the doorknob and opened the front door.

The sun filtered in through the curtains and highlighted hundreds of pictures of children that wallpapered the living room's walls from floor to ceiling. He locked the four deadbolts and then the doorknob. He removed his hat, set his equipment down, passed through the dining room, and walked down a short hall, which was also decorated with hundreds of images of children, and entered his bedroom.

The bedroom was no different when it came to his personal choice of decorating, but there was an addition of stacks of newspapers that stood about three feet high along the walls. He unclasped his suspenders and removed his long-sleeved shirt, tossing all—save for the suspenders—onto the floor. He pulled out a short-sleeved t-shirt from his dresser and slipped it on over his splotched potbelly. He stood before the streaked dresser mirror and fixed a skewed photo that was tucked into its corner. He rubbed his thick finger over it.

The people in the photo...

He remembered the day he took the photo. It was through his living room window. The young boy, the pretty lady, and the big dog all sat across the street from his house, exhausted from the summer heat it seemed. They rested. He watched and took pictures to remember the day.

...they were the same mother and son at the park.

CHAPTER NINETEEN

While Hogarth did his business, Benjamin listened to the crickets chirping around him. The scent of wildflowers wafted through the air. Darren jumped at a firefly that blinked in the darkness as if flashing Morse code. Benjamin gazed at the sparkling display above him. The stars covered the sky like millions of tiny pinpricks in black velvet. Hogarth lumbered up next to him and slid his snout beneath his hand. "Hey, Hoagie."

Darren took a seat next to Benjamin on the porch step.

"Nothing?"

"Nope." Darren held out his hands. "Nothing."

Hogarth made his way over to Darren and sat in front of him.

"Next time you'll catch one."

"Maybe I could use a net." Darren petted the dog's head. "Catch a whole bunch."

"Yeah, that would work, I guess."

"I could put them in a jar and it could be a cool nightlight."

"I don't think they would like that. Their mommies and daddies will worry."

"Yeah, I guess they would."

Hogarth sat content as if listening.

"Know what?" Benjamin said, tapping Darren's leg.

"What?"

"I had fun with you and your mommy today at the park."

"Me too, especially the ice cream after the park."

"Was good." Benjamin chuckled. "Wasn't it?"

The screen door creaked open and Aisha stuck her head out.

"Time for bed, honey."

"Okay," replied Benjamin.

"I was talking to my son, silly head."

Darren laughed as he got up. "Silly head."

Hogarth stood, his tail wagging.

"Good night, Benjamin," Darren said.

"Good night, buddy."

"I'm going to get ready for bed myself," Aisha said. "Coming?"

"In a bit," Benjamin said, standing.

"Okay." She closed the screen door behind her.

Benjamin rubbed Hogarth's head. "Need to use the bathroom again? Huh?"

A floodlight popped on above the barn door. Hogarth turned and released a low bark.

"It's just a light, Hoagie. A rabbit probably triggered its sensor."

A rumble escaped from Hogarth's throat, and he ran to the barn.

"Hogarth."Benjamin hurried after him.

The light cut to black, leaving them both in the dark. Hogarth stopped just before the barn door. The light kicked back on. His growl deepened. Benjamin grabbed him by the collar.

A crash of metal came from inside the barn. Benjamin held on tight to Hogarth as he lurched forward.

"Hogarth." Benjamin dug his feet into the ground. "Let's go in the house." Hogarth refused. "C'mon!"

Please! Help!

Benjamin's stomach dropped. The voice! It wasn't the man's voice, it was a girl's. And it *felt* real. Had it been real all along? Now wasn't the time to figure it out. He heard it. That's all that mattered, and he wasn't sticking around to find out.

"C'mon, Hogarth."

The porch light above the front steps flicked on. Aisha stepped out from behind the screen door wearing a pink bathrobe. "What's going on?"

Hogarth ran to her and sniffed her legs as Benjamin came up.

"Thought I heard something in the barn."

"Probably just raccoons or possums," she said.

"You're probably right."

The floodlight cut to black.

"C'mon, let's go inside," she said. "I gottaget up early and take Darren to his dad's."

"Sounds good."

As all three went back inside the house, Benjamin paused and stared out through the screen door at the barn before turning out the porch light. It could've been raccoons or possums, just as Aisha said, but his gut told him it was something more than just a wild animal.

CHAPTER TWENTY

He knew nothing about house repair. There was more to it than just nails and hammers. There were permits, knowledge, and experience. And plain old fix-it savvy, of which Benjamin had none. But under the circumstances, he'd have to cut corners, which meant he'd have to do things himself.

He needed to go through his dad's personal belongings still. Pack away memories, box up unwanted relics, and figure out what to do with the large collection of baseball cards. Could he find a buyer? Could he eBay them? Or keep them because his dad worked so hard collecting them?

House repairs. Bills.

They could be worth a lot of money and help in more ways than one.

The cards would have to wait, because he was about to attack the one thing he knew almost nothing about. Ripping out a wall. He figured tearing down a wall wasn't actually the hard part. He'd seen it enough on HGTV, and besides, tearing anything apart was always the fun part. He had a ten-pound sledgehammer, a crowbar, goggles, and gloves. With Aisha and Darren back home, this was the time to do it. Benjamin's only question about the wall was whether or not it was load bearing. He'd soon find out.

With his goggles and gloves on, he lifted the sledgehammer and rested it on his shoulder. He stepped up and stood in a batter's stance, pointed to the wall, and prepared for the pitch. A careful swing later, a hole the size of a softball appeared in the center of the wall. Another swing, another pit. Fifteen minutes later, Benjamin worked on a bottle of beer while resting his hand upon the handle of the sledgehammer, admiring his pockmarked work. His t-shirt was wet with sweat. His face and arms coated with a grayish white powder. The smell of mildew filled his nose and he covered it with the crook of his arm.

"Geez." He cleared his throat. "This will definitely open up the living room."

The top half of the wall was now a sort of spotted window. There were pieces of drywall that needed to be ripped away, but for the most part, it was complete. The lower foot and a half still needed some violent loving, but it could be torn away from the studs by hand.

Benjamin finished off his beer and removed his goggles. He squatted in front of the wall and removed a large piece of board and laid it on the floor. He then scooted down and took hold of another piece and pulled on it. It didn't come off as easy as the last; instead, it tore off into a large chunk.

The paper backing of the drywall ripped at an irregular shape. Benjamin didn't think anything of it, but when he flipped it over, the yellowish-brown paper with specks of black caught his attention. It was an old newspaper article that had been cut out. There was no date. The article had a black and white photo of a little girl, and at the top it read, "Halloween Horror Hits Home."

Benjamin sat down and read through the article until he came to the section where it ripped from the wall. He set it down and pulled the remaining piece from the stud. On its back, not only did it have the rest of the article, but it had another article next to it. This one also had a little girl's picture and no date. "Girl Next Door Gone Missing."

Benjamin tossed it down and pulled off another section. He swallowed hard when he saw more speckled articles glued to the backside. Once he pulled the rest of the drywall away, he counted nine articles in all. He sat there, sweating, not knowing what to make of them. He knew back in the day people would line the insides of their walls with newspapers for insulation. But this didn't seem like insulation to him. Old newspaper articles cut out and glued to the back of the drywall? This was too precise.

He took off his gloves and went into the kitchen for another beer. He twisted the cap off, leaned against the sink, and guzzled the cold liquid. He snapped the cap across the room and watched it hit the wall and bounce across the floor. Did the other walls in the house hide anything? He took another drink and nearly choked when a thought struck him. He slammed the bottle onto the counter and ran into the room that was now a haunted scrapbook and flipped over the first piece of drywall he tore away.

"Buffalo Boy Missing." "Morgantown Child Last Seen on Playground." "Murdered Mother's Missing Baby Baffles Police." "Family Christmas Turned Nightmare."

In the living room, Benjamin leaned against the couch and rested his forehead in the palm of his hand while staring at all the articles he spread out on the floor in front of him. Thirteen more articles, making the total twenty-two. All with pictures of the missing. All with no dates. All creating a swirl of questions inside his head he couldn't answer.

Please!

Benjamin perked his head. He listened. Eyes fixated on the articles.

Help me!

CHAPTER TWENTY-ONE

Aisha went through Benjamin's accumulated mail, most of which was credit card offers, bills, and an envelope that had only Benjamin's name printed on it in black marker. As she was about to open it, her cell phone wailed.

"Hello."

On the other end, a man's voice screamed, "Where in the hell are ya? You're supposed to be at home with Darren. It's my day to have him."

Aisha grabbed her head. "I'm sorry, Tyson. I had some errands to—"

"Y'know, maybe if you'd act like his momma instead of some bitch *girlfriend*, you'd think of more than just your damn self."

Asshole. Now you know why I left you.

"I said I was sorry."

"Where you at?"

"I'm at Benjamin's house."

"Shoulda known. I'm comin' over to get Darren."

"You know where Benjamin lives?"

"Yeah, I do. I'm not stupid."

The phone died on the other end, and Aisha hung up. Over on the couch, Darren watched television. She began to open the envelope with Benjamin's name on it when her cell rang again.

"What now? Haven't finished yelling at me?"

"Uh, no. Unless you want me to."

"I'm sorry, Benjamin. I answered without checking to see who it was. I thought you were Tyson. He's coming to get Darren. And, of course, he's pissed about something as usual. Says I'm playing your girlfriend too much instead of being a good mother."

"Guy's a real asshole. You're a far better mother than he'll ever be a father, or a man."

"So what's the call for?" she said. "Miss me?"

"Of course I do. No, I'm calling because while ripping out this wall—"

"It's a load-bearing wall, isn't it?"

"I'd prefer that, actually. No, I found some old newspaper articles inside it. Glued to the back of the drywall."

"That's nothing new. Lots of people did that back in the day to insulate their walls."

"Yeah, I know, but there's not enough here to consider it insulation. I wish it were. Trust me. I wish they were of plain old ordinary stories or of historical relevance, but they're not. They're much more interesting."

Her attention drew away to a black truck that pulled up in front of the house and parked in the street.

"No. These articles are of—"

"Tyson just pulled up. I gotta let you go. I'll see you in a few hours."

She slipped her phone into her front pocket as a knock came at the front door. She took in a deep breath, exhaled, and answered it. Darren ran up to Tyson and hugged him around the waist.

"Daddy!"

"How you doin', D-Man?"

"Okay," Darren said, letting go.

Tyson looked about the room. "This your pad now?"

She placed an arm out and rested her palm on the door jamb, blocking Tyson. "What's it to you?"

Tyson rolled his eyes. "Whatever."

He pushed past her and stepped inside the house.

"You excited about coming home with me, D-Man?"

"Yeah," Darren said.

"Why don't you go see if you have to use the potty," Aisha said.

"But I don't have to go," Darren said.

"Go ahead, honey."

Darren ran upstairs.

Aisha took a step toward Tyson.

"I'm with a man who loves me and treats me with respect, and you have the nerve to make a comment." Aisha stepped over to the door. "You drive around in a truck you can't afford and live in a slum of an apartment. And yet you still can't figure out why I have custody of Darren."

Tyson leaned in toward her, his face closer to hers, and said, "Not for long. *Bitch.*"

"And what do you mean by that?"

"It means you're a bitch. You don't need no fancy degree to know that."

"You know what I mean."

"You and your *boyfriend* may be doing better than me, but you still just a single momma who's *always* gone. Just bad parenting if you ask me. What I mean is I plan on having full custody of D-Man."

"What?"

Aisha's stomach dropped like a ton of bricks. Her nerves jolted and she felt her hands tremble. She swallowed back the heat that rose in her. Fought to keep her emotions from getting the best of her.

"You heard me. I want full."

"That'll never happen," she said with a crack in her voice.

"Yeah, well, you'll see."

She pointed toward the door. "Get out."

"Make me."

Tyson smirked.

Tears welled in Aisha's eyes.

"Don't make me call the police," she said.

"That raggedy threat don't work."

"I'm not going to do this in front of Darren." She gritted her teeth. "I said get out."

Darren came running down the stairs.

"Ready, baby?" She rubbed his cheek.

"Yep." Darren hugged and kissed her.

Tyson glared at her and said, "Let's go, D-Man."

"Bye," Darren said.

"Bye, honey." She reached out for him as he walked away with Tyson.

Right now, she hated the image of seeing her son hold that asshole's hand. She wrapped her arms around herself and felt her body shake. Her emotions were at the tip of her tongue. Tyson opened the back door and lifted him into his booster seat and strapped him in. Darren waved to her and she waved back. Tyson swung the door, looked back at her, and disappeared to the other side. The black Denali purred to life, swung around in the street, and drove away.

Aisha slammed the door shut, leaned back against it, and hit the door, balling.

He's not going to get... He won't get custody.

She hit the door again...

He can't!

...and screamed.

CHAPTER TWENTY-TWO

Tyson swung the black Denali into a parking spot at the Cloverfield Apartment complex. After cutting the engine, he hopped out, made his way around the truck, and opened Darren's door.

"We're going for a ride after I get some clothes."

He unbuckled him from his car seat.

"Where are we going?"

He set Darren on the ground and shut the door. "Gamma's place." He pressed a button on his key and the sound of the horn beeped from his truck.

"Gamma's!"

"Ya got it."

Tyson's apartment was small and a mess. Its living room and kitchen were one room, while a bathroom and a bedroom sat off a small hallway. Scattered paper lay on a bed that was the couch when it needed to be one. Empty beer bottles littered a side table. A large flat-screen TV sat in the corner on a glass console with an Xbox and a Blu-ray player beneath it. DVDs and CDs piled before it. Clothes lay about the floor like loose patchwork.

In the kitchen, Tyson grabbed a plastic cup, poured Pepsi into it, and handed it to Darren. He opened a cabinet and grabbed a box of Pop-Tarts, emptying one pack into his hand.

"This should hold you over till we get to Gamma's."

"Mommy doesn't let me have pop."

"Well, Daddy does. Go ahead and sit on my bed and eat. I gotta pack a few things."

In the bedroom there were twin-sized mattresses leaning against the wall on their sides, a small dresser next to them. Clothes were packed tightly in a closet that had no door. He pulled out two small suitcases and began throwing his and Darren's clothes into them. He then went into the bathroom and tossed in their toothbrushes and toothpaste.

In the living room, Darren sat on the bed and was wiping his hands and mouth with a bed sheet. Cup of pop on the side table, untouched.

"That's not a napkin, D-Man. That's my sheet. Go in the bathroom and use a piece of toilet paper."

Darren disappeared into the bathroom. "Can I have some water?" he shouted.

"I'll get you some on the way. Come on, let's go."

Before he opened the front door, Tyson pulled out two cell phones from his pocket, laid one on the side table, and tucked the other back into his pants.

"Why you got two phones?" Darren said.

"One's in case Mommy calls, the other's for…business."

"Which one's Mommy's?"

"Doesn't matter. C'mon, let's go."

On their way to his truck, a voice called out.

"Tyson! You got last month's rent? You need to pay up or I'll ship you out. Hear me? Tyson!"

He ignored the man as he buckled Darren into his seat. He pitched his luggage into the back, then hurried around to the driver's side and hopped in. Seconds later, the truck hummed to life and he pulled out, speeding away.

CHAPTER TWENTY-THREE

After his talk with Aisha, Benjamin thought if he cleaned up a bit it would take his mind off the articles. He made a large pile out by the barn with the rest of the drywall and returned the tools to their places. He wasn't the tools-in-the-trunk-of-the-car kind of guy. His dad had plenty to use.

He still hadn't gotten around to cleaning the barn. It was too much. And whenever he thought about making the attempt, his lazy bone usually spoke up and convinced him to do something else.

Hogarth padded into the barn as he lay the sledgehammer and crowbar back onto a well-abused workbench. He tossed his gloves, safety glasses, and some smaller tools into a wooden crate. He squatted and wrapped his arm around Hogarth.

"Why don't you clean this place up while I go take a nap, huh?" He patted the mastiff's furry, broad chest.

Hogarth drooled.

"I didn't think so. Well, I guess I can at least pull out the tractor and get a better sense of what needs to be done in here."

Benjamin climbed up onto its seat and rubbed its steering wheel, grinning. He'd always wanted to drive it, but as a young kid all he could do was stare at the hulking machine as it sat inside the barn. And that was his memory of the tractor. Staring at it. Now, he finally got to drive it. He checked the ignition, but the keys weren't there. He hopped out and went back to the workbench and looked inside old coffee cans filled with nails. Another can held bolts and nuts. Nothing. In front of him hung a large pegboard with hooks that held hammers, screwdrivers, pliers, and other various tools. Benjamin rested against the workbench and thought a moment.

"Stay here, Hogarth."

When he returned, he rattled a set of keys.

"Just as I thought. Dad's truck keys." Benjamin climbed up onto the tractor and stared at the controls. "I know nothing about tractors, but it's like driving a car, right?" He found the ignition and inserted a key that wore the John Deere symbol and turned it. Nothing. No rattle of the engine. No smoke billowed from its rusted smokestack.

It was dead.

"Now what?" He took the key out and thought for a moment. "Wonder if I can use dad's truck and pull it out. Use a rope or something and stick it in neutral? How do you put it into neutral?" He hopped off the tractor and pulled out his smartphone. "I bet Google knows."

With the tractor out, the barn wasn't as bad as he thought. It looked more like a storage unit than a country barn. There were boxes, gas cans, tires, and a riding lawnmower that had to be dragged out. Loose tools lay scattered about the hay-laden floor. The place needed to be organized.

Benjamin kicked at the hay. "I wonder how the floorboards are holding up in this place." He grabbed a rake standing beside the workbench and began pulling at the straw. He cleared a small spot and knelt to see if any rot had occurred. "Seems fine, but I really won't know until I get this hay cleared."

He decided the best spot to start at would be the far corner and crossed over to where the tractor had been sitting. His boot kicked into something that clinked, and he stumbled forward, catching himself before he kissed the barn floor.

"What the hell?"

He turned back and applied the rake. Its wiry prongs caught into something. He pulled it out, lay the rake down, and used his hands to clear away the spot. "I never knew this was here." He sat in a catcher's stance and grabbed a padlock that was attached to a trapdoor, sitting flush into the floorboards. Hogarth padded up next to him and sat. "This place is coughing up a lot of weird stuff. To be honest, I'm not sure if I really want to open this. What do you think?" The dog tilted his head. "I was afraid you'd say that."

He trotted out to the tractor and climbed inside. Seconds later he hopped out with the keys. On his knees, he tried several of them. None of them worked. He stuffed them into his pocket and spotted bolt cutters on the far wall.

"Who needs keys?"

Benjamin put the cutter to the lock and squeezed.

It snapped.

He removed the padlock and flung open the wooden door.

A makeshift ladder stretched down into the dark opening. Benjamin scanned the pegboard for a flashlight and didn't see one. Hogarth came up and sniffed around the opening.

"You wanna go first?"

Hogarth looked up at him, paused, and went back to investigating.

"Yeah, act like you're busy while I go down into who knows what."
Benjamin put his feet onto the ladder and eased himself down into the pit.

The smell of earth filled his nose.

His only light source coming through the square opening above him
broke into shards. Hogarth's large head peered down into the opening, his
ears hanging.

"I need the light. Go."

The dog didn't move. He stared and panted.

"Come on, buddy. Go!" He waved his arm at him. "Go. Shoo!"

Hogarth pulled back and disappeared.

He stepped off the ladder onto the floor. It was soft like putty.

"Pretty damn dark down here."

The air was cool and thick. He breathed heavy, and its asthma-like
sound deadened as soon as it escaped his lips. He took a few steps
forward with his jittery hand out in front of him. His stomach tumbled as
his imagination started inserting monsters hiding in the darkened corners
of the room.

"This is—"

His hand hit something and he jumped back.

"Holy crap!"

He swallowed hard. Trepidation held him in place. He inched his arm
out again, slow, slower, and grasped at the empty space before him. After
a second or two, his fingers touched it this time, but he didn't pull back. It
dangled at his fingertips. A string. He grabbed it. And when he was about
to pull it, he let it go. His heart felt like it was a bass drum, double-kicking
in time. His hand trembled. Benjamin felt warm, and after a wipe of his
forehead with his arm, he reached out for the string again, grabbed it, and
pulled.

A bright light blinded him.

He shut his eyes, squeezing them tight. He opened them and various
colors danced before him. Black spots floated. He blinked a few times.
The room became clearer, sharper. By the time his eyes fully adjusted, he
was already on his butt and hands scooting backwards across the dirt
floor, screaming.

Next to the ladder, he sat there frozen, staring ahead. What he saw
was sickening, and the yellowish light that shone from the bare bulb didn't
help. Benjamin's hands shook on his knees. Acid rose up into his throat
and he forced it back down. He squeezed his eyes shut to the nightmare.

This isn't real.

He inhaled a deep breath and exhaled.

He opened his eyes and snapped them shut again.

They're not real. They can't be.

When he opened them, the small bodies were still there. The pile of bodies at the far end of the cellar was real. Their skin was taut against their skeletal frames. Leather-like. Empty sockets stared back. Two of them had their mouths—still filled with little stained teeth—frozen open, as if their last cries for help were stuck in their throats. Heard on deaf ears.

"Oh. My. God."

In an instant, Benjamin hurried his way up the ladder and out of the earthen coffin and slammed the wooden door shut. "Holy shit! Kids?" He bent over, taking in deep breaths, and wiped his arm across his sweaty face. "Jesus!" Seconds later, he ran to the house.

? ? ?

After several hours and several empty beer bottles later, Benjamin sat on the living room floor and stared at the articles. *Gotta call the police.* The sections of drywall were lined up, leaning against the television console. No matter how many beers he drank, they didn't ease the pain or confusion. The shock. Fear. They didn't erase what those kids went through. They didn't stop his mind from racing with thoughts, questions. How did they get there? Who killed them? Why? He chugged the remainder of the bottle in his shaking hand, and tossed it onto the couch behind him without a care.

"Who in the hell would do that?"

He got up and paced the room.

"Children? Really?"

With his clammy palms, he wiped his eyes clear and pulled his cell from his pocket.

Gotta call the police.

He dialed 911, and before he could hit *send*, Aisha walked in through the front door with bags of groceries in her arms. Hogarth came trotting into the room from the stairs.

"I see you've been drinking," she said, heading to the kitchen. "And I see you got the tractor out of the barn."

Benjamin said nothing in return as she passed by without looking at him.

Hogarth followed and disappeared into the kitchen with her. "I stopped in town at the Park N' Shop and bought a few pizzas," she hollered. "Got pepperoni and plain cheese. Which do you want?"

Benjamin placed his cellphone back into his front pocket and sat on the couch in silence. Tears dripped from his eyes for company. It wasn't that he didn't want to tell her. He did. Real bad. He wanted to call the cops too. He wanted to run and scream. He wanted to do a hundred things all at once. He just didn't know *how* to tell her. So he waited. Waited for her to say something first. Anything. Something to force his words out.

Aisha entered the living room.

"Did you hear me?"

Benjamin wiped his face with his shaking hands.

"Oh my god, what's wrong?" she asked, sitting next to him. "What happened?"

Without looking at her, he said, "Remember..." He swallowed and ran his arm over his forehead, clearing away the beads of sweat he felt build there. "The articles... I, uh, I told you about?"

"Yeah, you said you found some old newspapers."

"No." He shook his head. "Uh-uh. No... I found articles about...about kids. Missing kids."

"What? I don't remember that part."

"*Those* kids." He pointed at the articles.

"I didn't even see these." Aisha grabbed one of the pieces of drywall and looked over the articles on it.

"This is—"

"I think I found them."

Her eyes widened. "Found...?"

He took the piece of drywall from her.

"*Them.*"

"Where?"

"Out in the barn. There's a...a grave beneath the floorboards," he said. "A cellar. Bodies."

"Please tell me you're kidding."

"Does it fucking look like I'm kidding?" he snapped. "Want me to show you?"

"We gotta call the police." She looked at the articles, and after a moment she covered her mouth with her hand. "Oh my god."

"What's wrong?"

"I gotta get Darren."

She ran into the kitchen and came back with her purse and dug into it. After a moment, she pulled out mail and her cell phone.

Benjamin stood from the couch. "Who are you calling?"

"Tyson." She handed him some envelopes and dialed the cell, tapping her foot.

"Why?"

"Damn, got his voice mail. Ty. I know you've only had Darren for a short while, but I'm coming to get him. Pack his things."

He grabbed her by the arm. "What's going on?"

"I was going to tell you later, but this—"

"Tell me what?"

"Tyson wants...full custody. He thinks I'm unfit as a mother. Can you believe that? Me? He threatened..." Without warning, she burst into tears. "He threatened to take Darren away from me."

"He can't do that! Hell, he can't *afford* to do that."

"What if he does?"

"He won't," he said, setting the piece of drywall back against the TV with the others.

"Between the articles, the barn, and Tyson's threat, I wanna make sure Darren's safe—and that's with me. I don't trust him." Aisha pocketed her cell. "Not since I caught him..." She wiped her eyes. "I just don't trust him, Ben, especially after his custody remark. I gotta go."

"Wait. You just got here. Let's call the police. Hell, I was about to right before you walked in." He grabbed her by the shoulders and looked into her eyes. "They'll handle this. Okay? No need to drive all the way back home."

"I can't." She pulled away. "I gotta get Darren." And she stepped over to the front door.

"He's screwed with you once, and if you go running back, he'll have the upper hand. None of *this* has anything to do with Darren."

"*Upper hand?*"

"If you go running back, he'll think he has control over you," he said. "And Darren's his leverage."

"I don't give a shit about any leverage," she said. "Call the cops. Show them what you found." She opened the door. "I'll be better once I have Darren with me. I'll be back."

Before Benjamin could state his case any further, the front door slammed behind her. *Damn it!* He tossed the mail Aisha gave him onto the couch, one envelope tumbling to the floor, and pulled his cell out from his pocket. Hogarth padded over to him, sat in front of him, and stared up at Benjamin, panting. "I'll pet you in a minute, I gotta make a—" The envelope lying on the floor grabbed his attention. It had no return address. No stamp. Only his name written in black marker.

He picked it up and took a seat on the couch.

"What's this?" Hogarth was now leaning against his legs, still waiting to be petted. "Maybe Aisha snuck this in as a surprise."

With his cell still in hand, Benjamin opened it, pulled out a folded piece of paper, and opened it. In cut-out letters, from what appeared to be from a magazine, it read, *Sell the farm or the boy will be taken! No cops!*

His breath hitched in his chest. For a moment Benjamin thought he was going to have a heart attack. The sense of nausea slammed into his head like a sledgehammer punching a hole into a wall. Fast and hard. Sweat beaded on his forehead. The letter shook in his hand. He let it fall to the floor and dialed 911.

As Benjamin waited on the couch, one thing looped over and over in his head. He couldn't shake it. He felt bad for even thinking it. The thought made him feel queasy.

Are the bodies in the barn there because—because of my dad?

Benjamin didn't have time to make it to the bathroom or even to the kitchen sink. Instead, he returned the contents of his stomach right there on the living room floor.

CHAPTER TWENTY-FOUR

It wasn't long after he cleaned up the mess, as best he could when a knock came at the front door. Hogarth stood before it and barked. Benjamin pulled aside the living room curtains. Outside in the gravel drive, a cruiser sat next to his car. A knock came again and he answered it.

"What kind of dog you got in there? A beast?" said a hefty older man. He squinted his eyes, which sat narrow in his head, making it look much bigger, rounder. His face gave the impression that he had eaten something sour. "Are you Mister Cole? I'm Sheriff Tucker."

"Yes, I am. Call me Benjamin. Please come in."

The sheriff hesitated and looked down at Hogarth.

"Come on, buddy. Upstairs. Go. Get up there," Benjamin said. The large dog lumbered up the stairs only to stop at the top and stare down at them. "He won't bite."

"Should get a saddle for that thing. Charge a nickel a ride. Probably get rich," said the sheriff as he stepped inside. "Thank you." He took note of the room. "Been drinking, have ya?"

"I had a few earlier."

The sheriff looked at him. "Looks like more than a few." He pulled out a small notebook from his breast pocket. "Now, you mentioned quite a few things in your phone call. Seems like you got your hands full. Let me see. You got a letter talking about a kidnapping, some newspaper articles, and you found a whole mess of dead children in your barn, right?"

"Yes."

"Looks like karma just crapped all over your garden. All this happening to you. Okay then. First, where's the letter?"

Benjamin glanced around the room. "You're pretty nonchalant about all this."

"Seeing is believing. You've been hitting the bottle. How do I know you didn't *drink* this all up?"

"It's right here." He picked it up from the floor and handed it to the sheriff. "I must've dropped it after I read it."

"Whoa, wait a minute," said the sheriff. He pulled out a pair of rubber gloves from his back pocket and stretched them over his chunky hands. "Don't want to contaminate…as you now have. Y'know, you should take care of evidence better than that. Hell, that creature you call a dog could eat this in one bite. Poof. No such thing as a letter. Got me?"

"I'll remember that."

"You bet."

Sheriff Tucker gave the letter a quick read.

"Where'd you get this? Out in your mailbox?"

"No, my girlfriend brought it from my house in Oakmont, PA. Small town outside of Pittsburgh."

The sheriff scratched his protruding belly, the buttons on his uniform fighting to hold it in place. "Let me ask you. How are you related to Mr. Cole that lived here? God rest his soul. No one gentler, I gotta say."

"He was my dad."

"Really? Never knew he had a son. You look nothing like him. No disrespect."

Benjamin took a step back.

"I've been told I look like my mother."

"Never met her," said the sheriff.

Feeling a bit uncomfortable, Benjamin said, "With all the things I told you about, shouldn't there be more officers?"

"This is Bradford, Mister—"

"Please. Call me Benjamin."

"All right. Well, since you're not from around here, Mr. Cole, let me tell you something."

"Actually, I was bor—"

"As I was saying, this is Bradford. It's a small town. Smaller than small, actually. We have more farmland and cows than roads and people." The sheriff started walking around, inspecting the room. More like being nosy, Benjamin thought as he watched the portly man. "And in Bradford we have less than two thousand folks who do nothing more than hit the ice cream stand on hot days or after a baseball win at the high school, go to the bars on a Friday night after a long week of work, and attend church on Sundays to make sure they've repented for closing down those very same bars two days prior. It's a simple town. Simple ideas."

Sheriff Tucker stopped at a large wet spot on the carpet in front of the couch, stared at it for a moment, and then continued back to Benjamin without missing a beat. "And to manage it all, along with the rest of the county, is the man that stands before you. And my deputy.

Deputy Rudnick. And right now, he's taking care of business elsewhere. Matter of fact, he *should* be here instead of me. There's a protocol, y'know. Kinda atypical for me to be here, but it's not unheard of. So, besides us, there's no one else. Matter of fact, when you called, I thought it might be a prank of some sort. But since you didn't come across as familiar and you gave me this address, thought I better check it out, seeing that Mr. Cole just passed."

"Okay then. So what do you think of the letter?" Benjamin said. "Should we be concerned?"

The sheriff took a step closer to him. "I'll send it off for analysis. I'll need your fingerprints too. That way we can exclude yours from this letter."

"Sheriff. Do you think it's a real threat? Something we should be worried about?"

"Where's your girlfriend now? She here in Bradford?"

"No, she's back home." Benjamin ran his hand through his hair. "Went to get her son, Darren."

Hogarth came down the stairs and into the living room and sat next to Benjamin.

The sheriff took a few steps away from him. "Serious about getting a saddle for that thing," he said. "You probably can tell I'm more of a cat person."

Who gives a shit if you like cats or goddamn gophers? Just tell me about the fucking letter!

"As I was saying, I'm gonna need to see your girlfriend. Ask her some questions."

"Fine. Okay. Whatever you need, but should we be worried about that damn letter? How serious is this? Should I go and get her and Darren? It's a freaking threat made out of cut-out letters, for crying out loud." Benjamin took a few steps away and came back to the sheriff, then rested his hands on his hips. "Sorry. But there's a lot of stuff going on here and my girlfriend is heading back to where that letter came from. For all I know, whoever made that," he pointed at the letter in the sheriff's hands, "they could be waiting for her *and* Darren."

Sheriff Tucker stared at Benjamin. "Nah, I wouldn't hold your breath on it. My gut tells me it's probably some sort of prank or someone wants to rile her up. She got any enemies?"

"None that I know of."

"She has a son. What about the boy's father? Any issues there?"

"He did tell her that he wanted full custody of Darren."

"See. He's probably messin' with her."

"I guess."

"Guess nothing." The sheriff pointed to the chunks of drywall. "Are these the articles you mentioned?"

"Oh. Yes," Benjamin said as he picked up a piece.

"Go ahead and set it back down, Mr. Cole." He held up his gloved hands. "Remember? Contamination?"

He put it back onto the floor. "Sorry."

The sheriff bent over and scanned a few of the articles. When he rose, his face was beet-red. An Oompa Loompa with a badge.

"Now you said you got some bodies in the barn?"

"Beneath the barn."

"Lead the way, son."

"I'd rather not, if you don't mind."

"I do mind. Show me."

? ? ?

As they entered the barn, Sheriff Tucker stopped and looked up, and then he looked at Benjamin. "Sorry about your dad. He was a good man."

There was a long rafter that spanned from the front to the back of the barn. It looked normal. Nothing out of the ordinary. However, it didn't take but a few seconds for the image of the deer to come to Benjamin.

Then his dad's body faded in.

His neck lay limp to the side as he hung from a noose that was tied off from above. With a sudden movement, his father's body bucked, eyes snapped open, bulging outward. His mouth fell open, and he screamed, "Don't come in here!" His voice was no longer soft, old. His words were like teeth being ground in a meat grinder. "Get out!"

Benjamin squeezed his eyes tight to the sight.

"You all right?" the sheriff said.

He opened them and glanced upward to the sight of his dad's body hanging from the rafter, swaying back and forth in his overalls. The rope creaking against the wood. Benjamin clenched his eyes tight, then eased them open to the lonely rafter.

"Can I ask you something?"Benjamin said.

"Sure?"

"Why would an eighty-three-year-old man hang himself?"

"I'm hoping an autopsy report will tell me that. Thinking your dad had some kind of terminal disease or something. Alzheimer's, maybe. He ever mention anything like that?"

And my wits…well, they come and go.

"Uh? No," he shook his head, "but I don't think he would've told me either."

"Pride will do that, and your dad had a truckload of it."

"What about the bodies? You think he—?"

"I've known your dad a lot of years. No way on God's green earth was he a killer." Sheriff Tucker glanced around. "Now, where's these bodies?"

Benjamin knelt and lifted the trapdoor. "I'm not going down there again."

The sheriff looked down into the hole. Light emanated from the bulb that Benjamin had left on when he scrambled out of there earlier.

The rotund man lowered his legs onto the makeshift ladder, squeezed himself through the opening, and disappeared.

"Holy smokes!" hollered the sheriff. "You're right. We got bodies."

"You talk as if you've seen plenty of dead people," shouted Benjamin.

"When you've been in a war, you have."

Benjamin spun around. Only twilight greeted him. This was what? The fourth, fifth, eighth time he'd heard the voice? Didn't matter how many times he'd heard it, it still spooked him. Drove him crazy.

In the living room window of the house, he saw Hogarth's face looking out at him, ears perked. He gave a silent bark.

Help me.

Benjamin took a step forward.

Another mimed bark from Hogarth.

Help me!

HELP ME!

"Help me!"

Benjamin jumped and turned.

"Help me, for cryin' out loud," said the sheriff, half-sticking out of the cellar at his chest.

"Oh, I'm sorry." Benjamin ran over to him, grabbed him by the hands, and pulled him out. "I didn't hear you."

"Thanks. Felt like I was in a bear trap." The sheriff removed his hat and wiped his forehead while he caught his breath. "Looks like you got some children down there. I counted nineteen of 'em."

Something flashed from inside the sheriff's hat.

The sheriff caught Benjamin's glance. "You see my little hideaway." He reached into his hat and pulled out a few items. "I have a band inside that I can tuck stuff into. Like this candy bar. According to my wife, I'm on a diet. What she don't know, and all that." He winked at Benjamin. "Hell, even my deputy don't know about this little hideaway." He held up a folded knife, its handle black with a silver edge. "My wife got me this True Utility lock knife from England or somewhere last Christmas. Fancy, huh? And then my lucky silver dollar."

"You fit all that inside your hat?"

"This ain't all I got. I can fit all sorts of things in there. I mean, I can't fit a firearm or anything really heavy or big, but yeah, it can hold several things."

"So…now what?"

The sheriff replaced the items and set the hat back atop his round head. "This is definitely more than our resources can handle. I'm gonna have to get a search warrant and get the state police out here."

"Search warrant?"

"Yeah, just can't be snooping around without the proper paperwork. Unless…" His brows raised. "I take it your dad owns this place, right?"

"Actually, no. He left it to me in his will. So I own it."

"Well, then. I won't need a search warrant if you give me the okay to search the premises."

"By all means, go ahead."

"Good. I'll call the state police. I'm quite positive they'll get a search warrant. Just in case. But they'll *forensically process* the scene." Sheriff Tucker quoted the air as he said this. "Bring in cadaver dogs, ground-sensing radar, and do a structured search of the entire property. Y'know, all that fancy stuff. I'll have my deputy call the hospital to clear some space."

"The hospital?"

"Don't have a county morgue, so the hospital's where they'll go."

"Do you need me still?" Benjamin said.

"Nope. This place will be locked down for the next two or three days. I want you to get a room at the Bradford Inn. Cozy little place. Not too pricy. Whenever I have family up, that's where I send them. So gather some of your things, because this place is about to get busy like ants at a picnic."

"I'd rather stay."

The sheriff took a step toward him. "What?"

"If I don't have to go, then I don't want to. This was my dad's farm and now it's mine. And whatever's going on here, I want to be here for it."

The sheriff rubbed his face. "Well, okay then. I can't make ya, but it's gonna get messy around here. Not to mention the reporters from our local paper. But I can keep them at an arm's length. Now, if any city reporters show up, I'm not sure how long I'll be able to keep them from you." He took another step toward Benjamin. "You sure you wanna stay?"

Benjamin nodded. "I can take care of myself. Besides, I've already seen the bodies. I think I can handle it."

I hope I can.

"All right, but I want you to call your girlfriend," said the sheriff. "Need to get you down to the station for those prints and to hear her side still."

? ? ?

Inside the house, Benjamin sat on the floor with a beer and his cell phone. It didn't matter that the sheriff was right outside. He needed it. He dialed Aisha's number. He'd tell her what the sheriff said, and that he thinks it's Tyson screwing with her, scaring her. He'd tell her about the night, and definitely tell her about the state police coming in. It rang three, four times, and then her voicemail answered.

"Wanted to fill you in on what's going on here. The sheriff thinks the letter is a scare from Tyson. He's probably right. Anyway…um…he's calling in the state police. Gonna get pretty busy around here. He said he wants us at his station, so he can fingerprint us and get your side of everything. Anyway, give me a call when you get this. Love ya."

CHAPTER TWENTY-FIVE

It wasn't long before the sun set upon Tyson and Darren. Headlights guided their Denali toward the Pennsylvania and Ohio border. In his rearview, he noticed that Darren had fallen asleep, and he turned down the volume of the current song that thumped within the cab. He hoped that D-Man would sleep the entire way to his mother's house. He didn't call her to tell her that he and Darren were coming. He didn't call Aisha either. Not that he needed to. Darren was his *goddamn* son too. He didn't have to let her know that he was taking Darren out of state for a few days. After their little argument back at her *boyfriend's* house, he figured she needed the scare. Maybe it would set her straight. What Aisha didn't know was that Tyson had no plans on gaining full custody of Darren. He couldn't afford to. And he didn't want to.

Just before the border, he pulled into the last rest stop in Pennsylvania before entering Ohio. Woods surrounded the desolate place. No other cars, or people, were at the stop. Only Tyson and his son. He pulled into a parking spot in front of a small building. An old soda machine sat sentinel between the entrances to the restrooms. After he put the truck into park, he glanced back at Darren, who continued to sleep.

"Hey, D-Man." He tapped his leg. "Gotta go to the bathroom?"

Darren didn't wake up. He slept soundly.

"Hang tough, I'll be right back in less than two shakes."

Tyson hopped out, hit the lock button, and eased the door shut so as not to wake Darren.

The rest stop was lit by three small lamps that gave off very little light. One flickered above the MALE entrance to the restrooms while the others were above the FEMALE entrance and above the soda machine. He tucked his hands into his pockets and shook a chill away.

It's like some fucking backwoods horror film.

He stopped at the soda machine, studied his choices, grabbed a dollar bill from his wallet, and returned his billfold after he slipped the buck into the money slot.

It spit it back out.

He pressed the dollar against his chest and flattened it, then tried again. Once again, it returned his George Washington. "Shit."He pocketed the dollar and stepped toward the men's room and paused when the lights of an oncoming car caught his attention. It parked a few spots away from his truck. Through the darkness, he could tell it was an old wagon. Its shape gave it away. *Don't see cars like that anymore.* It cut its lights, followed by the dying rumble of its engine.

Pretty cool.

Tyson glanced at his quiet truck and went into the bathroom.

An odor of ammonia punched him in the nose as he walked up to one of two urinals on the far wall. He unzipped his pants and began to relieve himself when, outside, he heard the soda machine's dollar slot buzz. Then buzz again.

He chuckled, knowing that whoever was trying to buy a Coke or Dew was in for a battle, since it wouldn't take his own dollar.

It buzzed again.

"Good luck with that," he said over his shoulder.

Then nothing.

Shit. It worked.

Then the *clunk* of the can dispensing from the machine.

"Man, you're gonna have to tell me your secret."

At his ear, a can of soda cracked opened.

He jumped. He hadn't heard anyone enter the bathroom. He stopped himself from finishing his business and before he could say a word, or zip up, his head was slammed forward, hard, into the cinderblock wall before him. His forehead hit against its rough surface. A pain jolted through his head, followed by a trickle of something wet slipping down onto his face.

"What the fuck, man!" Tyson said. "What's goin' on? My wallet's in my back pocket. Take it."

The sound of a soda can hit the floor.

He tried to turn his head and get a glimpse of whoever it was that held him against the urinal and wall.

A gloved hand released his head. Tyson eased himself from the wall. Heat flushed his face. He gritted his teeth, balled his hands into fists.

"What the fuck did I do?! Huh? What? You like robbing people at the pisser? Takes a real man to—"

The hand grabbed his neck and thrust his face against the wall. The cinderblock scraped his cheek. More wetness. More blood. Then, the wetness ran down his leg and the pungent smell of urine bit his nose.

"Shit! Look. Take my fucking wallet, okay? Take it. I've got a kid, man."

His wallet remained in his back pocket. Whoever held him didn't bother to take it.

"Please. Just take the cash."

From the corner of his eye, a silver flash came down. He screamed. White heat caused the muscles in his back to tense. A sensation of tearing and the vibration of metal against bone caused him to feel lightheaded. He coughed. Every breath he took caught short in his throat. An arc flicked by, and the pain jabbed his side. His legs buckled. He grabbed onto the urinal for support, to keep himself from falling to the piss-stained floor. The wetness had come again. It was at his back and his side, his kidney. The room tilted. He was weak. And with every plunge the silver blade made, he found himself fading away. He fell to his knees.

The gloved hand gripped his hair and pulled his head back. Everything was a darkening blur. He couldn't make out the simplest features. At his ear, three words stabbed him one last time before he was let go and collapsed to the floor.

"Your son's mine."

CHAPTER TWENTY-SIX

Yesterday when Aisha drove home to get Darren, she was able to calm her nerves during the drive. That didn't mean her feelings about it changed. It meant that she was better prepared for the oncoming fight. After listening to Benjamin's message earlier this morning, she couldn't believe all the stuff that was happening at the farm, and that Benjamin was staying. With her focus on Tyson, she called his cell several times while she drove to his apartment. She pulled into the complex's parking lot and swung into a spot in front of his building. She hopped out and scanned the lot for his Denali. It wasn't there. She ran to his door and knocked. No one answered. She called his cell again. From inside his apartment, it rang out an old Eminem song. She ended the call and hammered on the door.

"Tyson!" She fidgeted with the phone in her hand. "It's me, Aisha. Tyson!"

She ran around the building to the apartment complex's office. An old man sat behind a desk scattered with papers, coffee cup in his hand. "I'm closing up shop for an hour. Haven't had breakfast yet. Come back later." He took a sip and released a loud smack of his lips.

"Can you let me into an apartment? It's important."

The old man set his coffee down. "Whoa. No can do. Can't enter apartments less it's a maintenance problem or with consent from the resident of said apartment."

"Please." She stepped forward and placed her hands onto his desk, leaning into it. "His truck isn't here, but—"

"'Fraid not." He took another sip of his coffee and released another lip-smacking endorsement. "What apartment you talking about anyway?"

"9-C."

"You tell that cheap bastard he still owes me last month's rent. Or he'll be packing more than just the luggage he had yesterday."

"You saw him?"

"Yeah. Left with his little one."

"Shit!"

"Best not be skipping out on me. That fancy truck of his will be mine before he knows it."

Aisha ran out of the office.

"You tell him I want my rent," the man yelled.

She rushed back to his door and pounded. "Tyson!" Aisha cupped her hands over her mouth. She pounded again. "Tyson!"

The sound of the neighbor's door opening turned her around. A little boy's head peeked out. He was a handsome little guy, looked a little like Darren, with the same round eyes but a few years older. The boy stared at her for a moment, and then shut the door.

Aisha ran back to her car and climbed inside. She slapped the dashboard over and over and over again, screaming, shaking her head in a wild manner. All her frustrations were being beaten into the car. She bawled as she gripped the steering wheel with her stinging palms and squeezed until they ached. Her chest heaved as tears poured from her eyes. Her head throbbed as she cried for her only son. Letting go of the steering wheel, she leaned back and buried her face into her hands. Aisha felt helpless, scared. She took in deep breaths. Through blurred vision, she saw the little boy watching her from a window. His face was unhappy, as if he felt sad for her. He held up his hand and gave her a slow wave, and then looked back over his shoulder and disappeared behind the curtain. Aisha wiped her nose with the back of her hand. Her gut told her Tyson had made good on his threat. Instead of lawyers, he ran off with Darren.

She dialed Benjamin and took account of herself in the rearview mirror. He answered before she could finish wiping her eyes.

"Aisha," he said. "Glad you called. Did you get my message yesterday? This place is—"

"Tyson isn't home," she blurted. "I can't get hold of him. His phone's still in his apartment, because I can hear it ringing inside when I call. He was serious about taking Darren from me."

"You sure he's just not at a friend's house or something?"

"I talked to his landlord, and he said he saw Tyson and Darren leaving *with* luggage. I didn't even know Tyson owned luggage."

"Son of a bitch," Benjamin said.

"He's made good on his promise, Benjamin. I know it. *Feel* it!"

And with that, Aisha remembered why she left him two and half years ago.

She, Darren, and Tyson were living in Shady Side. A large four-bedroom condo near the popular Walnut Street where fancy restaurants, expensive shops, and bakeries lined its short drive.

It was Tyson's day off from Toofers, the clothing store he worked at in downtown Pittsburgh. Aisha decided to take a half-day from work and surprise Tyson and Darren. Maybe hit the ice cream shop down the street from them. But that all changed when she discovered Tyson in their bed with another woman.

She didn't remember how it all went down. Only that Darren cried in his room. Glass smashed into walls. Tyson stood between Aisha and the naked girl. It was a blur.

"Call the police," Benjamin said.

    "I don't know what—"

    "Call the police!"

CHAPTER TWENTY-SEVEN

"I definitely prefer riding around in an unmarked car, don't you?" Eddie said. With his arm hanging out the passenger side window, he patted its door. "Nothing like the old Malibu."

"Yeah, the cruisers are kinda stuffy," Carl said.

The afternoon air was hot against Eddie's face. A teenage boy with a tall, green mohawk rode a skateboard down the sidewalk.

"If you don't mind me asking, how are things at home?"Eddie said.

"Empress Palpatine continues to rule the empire, if that's what you're asking," Carl said.

Eddie couldn't help but laugh. "So, does that make you Vader?"

"I wish. I'm a second-rate Jar Jar Binks at best. Our dog, Sophie, would be Vader. There's a hierarchy, y'know."

Eddie continued to chuckle. "I'm sorry. I don't mean to laugh. It's just you make it sound so bad."

Carl glanced at him. "I'm sleeping on the couch."

"Oh," Eddie said.

"In the basement."

"That bad, huh?"

"Yep."

"Sorry."

"No need. Not your fault."

They turned the corner, and Carl pointed to Eddie's side of the road. "Look who I see." The waitress from the Oakmont Grill was walking down the sidewalk toward them. The car slowed to a crawl.

"What are you doing?" Eddie said.

"Nothing."

She noticed Eddie and waved.

Carl pulled over to the curb and put it into park.

She came up to Eddie's window and peered in.

"Hello."

"Hello," Eddie said.

"Hi there," Carl said."I'm the sidekick. Detective Haines."

"Oh, I didn't know you guys were police officers."

"Detectives," Carl said.

"Okay, detectives. I thought you were insurance salesmen with the suits and all." She giggled, covering her mouth. "I'm so sorry."

"That's okay and funny." Carl's shoulders shook as he laughed.

Eddie chuckled and leaned forward. "I'm Detective Lane. Eddie Lane."

"Nice to meet you, Mister... or Detective Lane. I'm Tabitha. Waitress, Chapman. Since I'm off-duty, you can call me Tabby."

"Okay, Tabby," Eddie said.

Carl leaned over and said, "You two should go out sometime."

Eddie covered his face as the feeling of embarrassment flushed his body. "Carl."

"Was it something he said?"

Eddie removed his hand. "It's just..." He took a quick glance over at Carl, who sat there with a smile from ear to ear, proud of his love connection. "My partner means well, but he's clueless for a detective." His cell rang. "One moment, please." He snatched it from his belt.

Tabby took a step back.

"Detective Lane. Oh? Okay. Of course. I know the street. Yes, sir. We're on our way."

He ended the call and clipped the cell back to his belt.

"We gotta go, Carl. Like right now!"

"Gotcha."

Carl threw the car into gear, and he checked his side view mirror.

With his attention back to Tabby, Eddie said, "I'm sorry."

"That's okay." She smiled. "I understand. Bye."

"Bye."

The Malibu swung out into traffic. As Eddie watched her grow smaller in the side mirror, the car's sirens chirped as it picked up speed. He felt bad, but it wasn't meant to be. Seconds later, she disappeared as they turned onto a side street.

CHAPTER TWENTY-EIGHT

In the photo, Darren sat against a tropical backdrop. His elbows propped up on his knees. A smile painted from one ear to the other. His eyes bright with happiness.

"This...this is the most current photo I have of him," Aisha said. "Had it taken at...People Pictures in Squirrel Hill. About a month ago."

She blew her nose into a Kleenex and balled it into her hand.

"Thank you, Ms. Jones," said Detective Lane.

She watched the detective study the photo as he stood by the front door in his steel-blue suit and black necktie, briefcase in hand. His black, wavy hair was short and framed his brown-skinned face nice and neat.

He looked up and said, "He's a handsome boy."

"This Tyson," said Detective Haines. "Is he an ex-husband or ex-boyfriend?"

"Ex-boyfriend," Aisha said. "Thank God."

"Wasn't the marriage kind, huh?" said Lane.

Aisha shook her head.

Detective Haines flipped a page of his small notepad and jotted down something with his pencil. "So Tyson never mentioned anything about taking a trip or visiting family?"

"No. Nothing. Besides, Darren would've said something to me about a trip or a family visit," Aisha said. "Here's the picture of Tyson." She handed Detective Lane a second photo.

He studied it. "Looks familiar. What's his last name?" He passed the photo to his partner.

"Price."

"Didn't we bust this guy for a DUI not too long ago?" said Detective Haines.

"That's it. Yeah, that's him," said Detective Lane.

Aisha straightened up on the couch seat. "DUI?"

"Pulled him over for drinking and driving in town," said Detective Haines.

"Was Darren with him?" Aisha said.

"No," said Detective Lane.

Detective Haines took a step closer to Aisha. "Was he a big drug hound? Boozer?"

"Honestly, no. I know he drank, but…and never around Darren that I know of. Then again, what do I really know about him?"

"I know it's been rough." Detective Lane stepped over to her. "I can't imagine what you're going through. We appreciate you answering our questions, and for the pictures. We don't like to see missing kids, especially kidnapped ones. An Amber Alert will be put out ASAP." He took the photo from Detective Haines and placed it along with the one of Darren into his briefcase. "We see this kind of thing a lot. He probably took Darren to a friend's or family member's house. These types of cases are usually just misunderstandings." He handed her his business card. "Please don't hesitate to call if anything comes up. Any time."

"I will," Aisha said, looking over the card. "Thank you."

"Thank you," said Detective Haines.

She closed the door behind them, placed her back against it, and slid down to bent knees as thoughts of her son entered her mind. Birthdays. Christmases. His laughter filled her with tears and sorrow. The idea of Darren stolen from her, and especially by his own father, never ever crossed her mind. She knew Tyson was a self-centered son of a bitch who had cheated on her. But to kidnap his own son? *Her* son? She glanced over to the stuffed animals lying on the floor and let loose a faint smile as the tears continued to slip down her cheeks. Aisha couldn't imagine a life without her little boy.

CHAPTER TWENTY-NINE

For the past three days, the state police had done their work like busy bees. A black Suburban came and went, taking the bodies to the hospital morgue—a temporary holding facility with refrigeration units—until they could be taken by a contract ambulance service to a location better suited for the autopsies. They searched the premises with cadaver dogs and used radar to see if there were more bodies in the cellar of the barn. Nothing was found on both accounts. They asked questions that seemed to go on forever. In hindsight, Benjamin should've left. It was a madhouse. But now, the place was quiet again.

He hadn't done much throughout the day. A migraine that seemed to last the entire time the police were there kept him from any real thinking. Since Aisha wasn't back yet, he figured popping some aspirin and getting to bed early would do him some good. Tomorrow morning he would get back to the barn.

Tonight, he would sleep upstairs in his old room, on an actual bed instead of the worn couch. Hogarth followed him and hopped up onto the twin-sized bed.

"C'mon, buddy. On the floor. This bed's too small for the both of us."

Hogarth stepped off the bed and left the room.

"Don't be mad." The sound of the mastiff's paws thumped down the stairs. "The couch will be more comfortable anyway."

On the small nightstand, the hands of an old alarm clock read 11:16 PM. Benjamin clicked off the lamp light and lay on his belly, leg hanging off. He gave thought to the past few days. To the barn. To his dad.

How much did you know?

He closed his eyes for a few seconds, and then eased them open.

*What...what did you...*he yawned...*know?*

The alarm clock read 11: 23 PM.

He blinked, slow and slower.

Did you ki...? I need to...know.

It wasn't long before his headache fell away to sleep.

Please!

HELP ME!

Benjamin bolted upright, his breathing rapid.

Hogarth barked downstairs.

He took a moment to gather himself, then turned on the lamp. The alarm clock read 3:58 AM. Benjamin took the corner of his bed sheet and wiped his face. After he threw the sheets back, he went to the top of the stairs. Hogarth stared at the front door, a low growl rumbling beneath his breath.

"What's the matter with you?" Hogarth kept his eyes on the door and ignored his words. "You never bark to go out."

Benjamin got dressed, grabbed his car keys from the kitchen table, and went outside with Hogarth.

After the hive of action had hit the farmstead, everything still remained intact. The grounds weren't dug up. And since there were no close neighbors or media swarming the place, there was no police tape strung across the entrance of the barn. Everything was back to normal.

The tractor remained in front of the barn, looking like a large beast guarding it with all of its past secrets. Hogarth ran to it and the floodlight popped on when he entered. He barked. The entrance looked as if it were a flytrap, wide open, waiting for its victims to enter so it could snatch them up in one large bite.

"Hogarth. Come here," he said. "Crap."

Instead of going inside, Benjamin hurried to his car and started it. He backed it up and pulled it around so its headlights faced the barn. Through his windshield, he saw Hogarth scratching at the trapdoor.

"Gotta be kidding me."

The dog barked again.

"Seriously, this has to be a joke."

Benjamin hopped out and ran to him. He didn't do anything. He only stood there and stared at the trapdoor. His mind raced with crazy thoughts. Did they come back? Were the children waiting down there with bloodstained teeth? Hungry? Hogarth knew something Benjamin didn't, and Benjamin didn't like that.

Another bark.

"Get away from there."

Hogarth continued to scratch, splinters of wood tearing away.

Benjamin grabbed him by the collar and with nearly all his strength pulled him back. "Stay!"

Hogarth sat and whined.

Benjamin paced around. "Shit! Barking dog. Night time. Last time I went down there…" He glanced at the hatch door. "Shit. Okay, I'll call the sheriff. He'll come out here and… Shit…He'll think… What if there's nothing? What if you're just spooked? Huh, boy? You just barking at mice?" He rubbed his face. "Okay…shit…okay, I'm gonna go down there and face whatever's spooking you, and if anything happens to me, I want you to make like Lassie and get help." He stepped toward the door. "You ever heard of the saying 'nothing good happens after two in the morning'?" He reached down and grabbed the handle. "Well, this is a prime example of that."

Hogarth backed up, ears perked, jaw closed.

Benjamin swung the door open, and it fell backward against the floor. Dust kicked up into the air, particles dancing around in the beam of his headlights. Benjamin coughed and covered his mouth with his arm.

He leaned over and looked down into the darkness. He couldn't see anything. A part of him was expecting to see a zombie clambering up the ladder, chomping its teeth for a bite. Maybe a horde of them waited for him to come down where the world ran slower. Where nothing could hurt you. No marriage. No shitty job. Just death and the damp, cool earth beneath your weary bones.

"Well. Here goes nothing."

He climbed downward and disappeared into the pitch.

???

Benjamin inched toward where he thought the pull string was and outstretched his arm to grab it. He was sure he had reached it by this time before, but instead of finding the string, his foot kicked into something.

He froze.

Various images flashed through his mind; everything from *Night of the Living Dead* to *Poltergeist*. He shivered when he thought of the pool scene where the muddy caskets and skeletons popped up from beneath the water's surface. Benjamin tapped his foot against it. It was solid but gave a little. Kind of soft.

With both hands he reached up and felt the air above his head. His fingers caught the pull string. He covered his eyes and yanked it. Light seeped in between his fingers.

Benjamin removed his hand…

…and at his feet lay Tyson's body.

He startled and stumbled backward until he hit the ladder.

"Shit." He cupped his mouth and stood there. Staring. "Shit! Shit! Shit!"

Tyson's eyes and mouth were open. Dried blood speckled his teeth, splattered his face, and covered his arms. The entire side of his shirt—the kidney area—was covered with numerous holes and a large dried stain.

Benjamin knew Tyson, met him a few times, but he never really *knew* him, and he never wanted to. But still, he couldn't help feel sorry for him. He may not have been the best husband, or person, but he did his best for Darren, and for that he respected him. A little.

CHAPTER THIRTY

"You got yourself a real house of horrors here, don't you?" Sheriff Tucker yawned. "I'm starting to think you're either bad luck or you're the killer." He checked his wristwatch. "And a quarter after five is too early for killing, don't ya think?"

"What? No. No. I'm not the killer," Benjamin said. "Blame the bad luck. Not me." He wiped his hair. "Really."

Outside the entrance to the barn, a police cruiser pulled up and parked next to the sheriff's Bronco.

"What the hell?" said the sheriff.

A young man in his late twenties climbed out and waved.

"What are you doing here, Deputy?" hollered the sheriff.

"Just popping in to see if you need any assistance," he said with a crack in his voice. "Called the hospital. An ambulance is on its way to pick up the deceased."

"That's Deputy Travis Rudnick," Sheriff Tucker said. "Couldn't find his ass if it farted in his face."

Benjamin chuckled.

"Everything's fine here. All under control," shouted the sheriff. "Go ahead and start your day by patrolling the town."

"Think I'll *patrol* some donuts from Vinnie's Bakery." He chuckled. "Want me to bring some back for you?"

The sheriff shook his head and sighed. "Just go do your duty, will ya?"

"Yes, sir, will do," replied the deputy, dejected. He climbed back in his cruiser, backed up, and drove away.

"Jesus criminy." The sheriff rested his hands on his hips. "Okay. Here's what I want *you* to do," he said, pointing at Benjamin. "I want you to go inside that house of yours, and I want you to stay there. If you even go to the grocery store, I wanna know. You take that monster you call a dog out for a piss, I wanna know. You take a shit, I wanna know. Got it?"

"I do," was all that Benjamin could say. The sheriff's tone told him enough to know that a smart comeback would be stupid.

As Benjamin headed to the house, the sheriff called out to him, "And tomorrow, I want you and your girlfriend at my station."

"Okay, Sheriff."

"Know what? I don't want ya here," said Sheriff Tucker. "I want you to get a room at the Bradford Inn."

"Why? I stayed—"

"There's no arguing this time, Mr. Cole! You have another body on your premises. So I suggest you gather some of your things, or I'm gonna give you a nice comfy cot in a nice comfy cell to sleep on. I'm shuttin' this place down."

CHAPTER THIRTY-ONE

When the mailbox clanked outside Aisha's front door, she awoke with a jump and sat up on her leather couch. She stretched and checked the clock on the far wall.

"Too damned early."

With a big yawn, she found her way to the bathroom mirror and stared. Bags big enough to carry groceries hung beneath her eyes. Her hair tangled. Most of her makeup rubbed off on the couch, she presumed.

What kind of mother are you? You let your only child slip away. You let him go.

She turned her back to the mirror.

"It's my fault."

She tore a small strand of toilet paper off the roll and wiped away the tears that bubbled up in her eyes.

After she threw the tissue into the trash, Aisha searched the refrigerator for something to eat. It revealed a mixture of outdated food and less than appetizing items for breakfast. Condiments hadn't caught on as a breakfast-for-champions kind of meal yet, and neither did an old carton of milk. Seeing that good old American cheese stays good for an unknown amount of time, she grabbed a piece, removed it from its wrapping, and ate it in two large bites as she made her way to the front door.

The Sunday edition of *The Post Gazette* lay on her welcome mat that read *Wipe Your Damn Feet!* She stood in the doorway and flipped through it until she came to a pile of ads, letting the cool breeze caress her face.

It took her a few moments once she found the ads to notice the letter sticking out of her mailbox. She grabbed it, stepped back inside, and shut the door behind her. The envelope was plain save for one word.

MOMMY.

She dropped the newspaper to the floor and tore open the envelope. She knew exactly what was inside.

It wasn't written with cut-out letters; instead, it was written in red crayon. As she read it, her hands shook. Tears brimmed and fell from her eyes. From inside her purse, her cell rang, startling her. "God." After pulling it out, she answered it.

On the other end, Benjamin's voice came through.

"Hey. You on your way? There's something I need—"

"I got another letter," she said.

"What? What did it say?"

Aisha broke down and sobbed into the phone.

"What did it say, Aisha? Tell me."

"Says, 'You'll never see your boy again.'"

"What the fuck?!" Sniffling came from Benjamin's end of the line.

She wiped her face with her hand and said, "I gotta call Detective Lane."

"Who?"

"He's the detective I spoke to yesterday. I was gonna tell you all about it when I got to the farm."

A large sigh came through.

"What?" she said.

"There's something else." Silence. "The reason I called... I didn't want to tell you this over the phone, but..."

"Just tell me, Benjamin. What is it?"

"In the barn, the cellar, last night. I found Tyson's body."

Aisha didn't move. Her throat tightened, her heartbeat rattled against her chest.

"Aisha?"

She sat on the couch. He was dead. It's something she didn't wish on him, no matter how he treated her in the past. But the news didn't hit her hard. She wasn't shocked by it. She was surprised, though. Surprised that he was found at the farm. No tears fell from her eyes. Then a thought caught her breath.

"Aisha?"

"Was Darren with him?"

"No."

"Oh, thank god." A moment passed, and then another realization hit her. "Darren *really* was kidnapped. Oh my god." She shot up from the couch. "Oh my god!" She cupped her forehead with her hands. "Oh my fucking god! What did I do, Ben? What did I do to deserve this? What did Darren do?" Aisha kicked the couch with her bare foot. "This is a nightmare."

"Listen to me," demanded Benjamin. "I want you to call the detective again. You hear me? Tell him everything. Okay? Aisha?"

"Y-yeah." She wiped her face with her hand. "Jesus."

"After you talk to the detective, come straight here, okay? I don't want you to be alone. Honestly, I don't want to be alone."

"I will."

"I'm at the Bradford Inn. Not the farmhouse. Room eight."

"You're at a hotel?"

"Sheriff's orders. And when you get here, we have to go to the station. I'll explain later," he said. "Call the detective."

???

"Besides this letter, have you noticed anything else out of the ordinary?" Detective Lane handed the letter to Detective Haines.

"My boyfriend found Tyson—"

"The DUI guy?" said Detective Haines, looking up from the letter.

"Yeah. He was found dead."

"Dead?" said Detective Lane. "When?"

"Last night." Aisha sat on her couch and rubbed her foot. It was red and sore from kicking the sofa earlier. "My boyfriend found his body up on his farm in Bradford."

"Certainly takes him off as our prime suspect, doesn't it?" said Detective Haines.

Detective Lane looked at Detective Haines, and then back at Aisha. "What's your boyfriend's name?"

"Benjamin."

"Last name?"

"Sorry. Cole. Benjamin Cole."

"Was…?" Detective Lane let the remaining words fall away.

"No, my son wasn't found," Aisha said. "But there's more. There have been others."

"Others?" said Detective Lane. "What do you mean?"

"Before Tyson, some children were found," she said. "Benjamin was tearing out a wall at the farm—"

"Is this farm your boyfriend's?" said Detective Lane. "Property?"

"It was left to him," she said. "He found a whole bunch of articles that were glued to the back of the drywall. All the articles were of missing children. Abducted. Then while clearing out the barn, he found a hidden door in the floor, and when he climbed down into it, he found the children."

Detective Haines said, "The same ones from the articles?"

"We think so."

Detective Lane turned toward Detective Haines and said, "I want you to call the Bradford Police Department and find out who's in charge up there. Get any and all info on Tyson and those children. Where they took them, everything." He looked at Aisha. "We're gonna need to talk with your boyfriend too."

"I'm heading there now," she said. "Actually, I'll be staying at the Bradford Inn. Room eight. He said the sheriff shut down the farm."

"Okay. Sounds good. I'll see what's going on up there, so expect to see me up there soon," said Detective Lane. "If I find out anything, I'll let you know."

Detective Haines stepped forward. "Just so you know, the Amber Alert will stay in effect until we find your son. We're doing our best. I promise."

Aisha gave a faint smile and nodded.

"Don't let us hold you up," said Detective Lane. "It's best to be with your boyfriend, someone who loves you right now. Even though it seems that no matter where you go, there's…"

Aisha didn't say anything and let Detective Lane catch himself.

"Anyway, we'll let you go."

After they left, she headed for Bradford.

CHAPTER THIRTY-TWO

After they met with Sheriff Tucker at the station, Benjamin and Aisha lay naked beneath the sheets and hugged one another, neither one letting go first. They'd been through a lot in their own way. They both pulled away. Benjamin wiped her eyes, and then cleared his own. He palmed her cheeks and kissed her. He rested his chin atop her head as she buried her face into his chest. With one hand on the back of her head and the other around her waist, he held her and didn't want to let go.

She threw the sheets off of them.

At the sight of her body, a rush of heat spread through his body. He took her all in. His heart thumped. He pulled her closer, tighter.

Aisha ran her fingernails through his brown hair, dragging them across his scalp. He closed his eyes in response and felt her lips on his. She rolled on top of him, reached down between them, and adjusted herself, and he moaned. Together they worked as one, their motions complementing one another. Fast. Slow. Faster. Slower. After some time, his body clenched. Her thighs clenched tight. With their dance over, Aisha lay down on top of him. Her breasts and stomach cool with sweat. They both sighed and fell asleep together.

CHAPTER THIRTY-THREE

The next morning, Aisha sat in bed with a cup of motel-made coffee and watched television while Benjamin took a shower. She was tired from the excitement they'd had and from last night. With her feet tucked beneath her, she took a sip and let the cheap caffeine fill her stomach with warmth and energy that would be needed to get her through the day. She wasn't a big coffee drinker, but this morning she needed it.

She scanned the channels and decided on a local news station that was giving their top-of-the-hour news brief.

The news anchor reported that a man in Bradford by the name of Eugene Greely was arrested in the woods of Swan Park for taking photos of children while they were at play. A parent spotted him and immediately called the authorities.

A roadmap of thoughts intertwined through Aisha's mind. She and Darren and Benjamin were at that park not long ago. Was this man there too? She swallowed hard at her next thought. Did he have anything to do with Darren's abduction and Tyson's death? Or the children in the barn cellar?

She set her coffee on the table beside her, hopped out of bed, and burst into the bathroom.

"Whoa, shut the door," Benjamin said. "You're letting out the warm air."

"I know who took Darren!"

???

"He could be the one behind the letters," Benjamin said. "Behind it all. Those children in the barn. Tyson. He probably has Darren."

Aisha grabbed his hand. "It *has* to be him."

Benjamin cupped hers. "They caught the son of a bitch."

Seconds felt like hours as they sat on the bed, Hogarth lying behind them.

"They have to have more info than what was on the television," Aisha said. "You gotta call the sheriff."

"Actually," Benjamin said, "I think calling Detective Lane would be better. He's the one handling Darren's case." As soon as he finished the sentence, the words sounded ugly. *Darren's case.* "Just makes sense."

Without a word, she grabbed her cell and called.

And as she did, Benjamin pondered an idea. One he had considered, but now must do. Sell the farmstead. Tie up the loose ends and sell the place. It was becoming too much to handle. It wasn't what he wanted to do, but what he *had* to do. He'd call Uncle George and see if he'd still be interested in buying it from him. Warts and all.

He would wait to tell Aisha his plan. Right now, the man who kidnapped Darren and killed Tyson—and all those children—was apprehended, and that was the best news he'd heard in a long time. But still, there was no time to throw excitement to the wind.

"Okay." Aisha's face wore a look of defeat. "Thank you."

"What did he say?"

"He said he couldn't give me any information the local news didn't already have. He'll call if he learns anything."

"That's it?"

"Yeah." She sat on the edge of the bed. "We need to stay strong, though."

Benjamin rubbed her back. "I know."

"Things have to get better, don't they?" she said.

"They will."

CHAPTER THIRTY-FOUR

The next afternoon, a knock came at the motel door. Aisha peeked through the peephole, saw Detective Lane standing in a gray suit with his briefcase in hand, and opened the door.

"Detective Lane."

"I was beginning to think no one was here."

"Please, come in," she said.

"Thank you." He looked about the room. "Nice dog." He pointed to the bed, where Hogarth slept and snored.

"He must be tired. Usually he's at the door before me."

"Where's your boyfriend? Benjamin, was it?"

"He's at the cemetery." She shut the door. "See you made it to Bradford."

"Yeah, came up yesterday." He smiled. "I wanted to make a personal trip over here to tell you some news about this man they busted over at Swan Park."

"What did they find?"

Detective Lane held up his briefcase and pointed to the bed. "May I?"

"Sure, he won't wake up. He's out."

Detective Lane set his briefcase down, opened it, and pulled out a manila folder. "Our suspect is cooperating. That's the good news. The bad news is we've discovered thousands of photographs of children in his house."

"Thousands?"

"Yeah. He wallpapered his bedroom and hallway with them. Living room too."

She sat on the edge of the bed. "My god."

"That's not all." From the folder he pulled out several pictures and handed them to her. "We found these among them."

She palmed her mouth.

The first one she looked at was of her, Darren, and Hogarth sitting in grass.

"You okay?" said Detective Lane.

"Fine. I'm fine."

"You sure?"

"Yeah, I'm sure," she said.

"Do you remember anything about that one?"

Aisha thought a moment. Her head pounded the beat of an oncoming headache. She squinted. "I don't think so. Should I?"

"That depends. This photo was taken of you three while you were sitting across the street from the suspect's house."

She looked at him. "Are you sure?"

"Positive."

"I really don't remember what day this was."

"It's okay. I'm not interrogating you." He smiled. "What about the others?"

She glanced at the other photos.

"These were definitely at the park."

"I figured as much," he said. "I definitely think we have our man. Have to build a solid case against him, and once we do, hopefully all the cold cases we have on those other missing children will be solved. And you'll have your son back."

Aisha gave him a small smile as he took the photos from her. "Is that a promise?" She clasped her hands together before her. "There are a lot of parents out there still waiting for answers."

"Don't worry. You won't be left without answers."

"You didn't answer my question."

"All I can say is that I'm not giving up, and neither should you."

"Do you have children?"

"No, I don't," he said as he packed up his briefcase.

"It's the best thing in the world," she said.

Detective Lane opened the motel door.

"And the scariest thing in the world," she added. "You're in constant fear for them. Over everything. Anything. So when a parent asks for a promise that their only child will be found and safely returned, she expects a better answer."

"I promise."

"Thank you."

He stepped out of the room. "By the way, you guys are free to go back to the house. No sense staying in this tiny room if you don't have to." He smiled and shut the door behind him.

CHAPTER THIRTY-FIVE

When Benjamin got out of his car, he saw Uncle George standing at his dad's grave. He weaved between headstones and markers—making sure not to walk across what appeared to be a fresh burial—and said, "Uncle George."

His uncle turned, spread his arms, and hugged him.

"Looks like Dad's getting a lot of visitors today."

"If two is a lot, then yeah, he is." George chuckled.

"I didn't see your car."

"I'm parked on the other side," said George.

Together, they stepped to the grave.

"How are you?" said George. "With that circus at the farm and all?"

"You saw that, huh?"

"Drove by the other night. Figured it'd be best to stay away. Lucky for you we got a small local paper around here. Nothing like the big cities or anything. So there's not a whole lot in there about what's going on. I'm surprised you haven't gotten any calls from Pittsburgh about it since you're a journalist and all."

"Actually, me too. Although it never crossed my mind."

That was the truth. Benjamin never thought about any of his contacts calling him from the newspapers he'd done freelance for. Maybe he was too close to it all. The actual victim. And so he couldn't be the interviewer. In the end, though, it didn't matter. He wouldn't tell them anything anyway.

Benjamin bent over and wiped away a few leaves and blades of grass from the face of his dad's stone. He stood and arched his back. For a brief moment, he wondered if he should mention the voices or not. He didn't think his uncle would consider him crazy, but he wanted to know if he had ever heard them too. Or if his dad heard them.

But instead of asking him about the voices, he decided to ask him an even bigger question. One that had been on his mind for a while.

"Can I, uh, ask you something?"

"Sure. Anything."

"This is hard, but, uh, did my dad have anything to do with those kids found on the farm?"

His uncle's face wore a look of shock. His eyes wide, mouth open.

"Are you serious? Joking, right?"

"No, I'm not. Did he put those kids there?"

"Mind my words, but *hell* no." He grabbed at his forehead and ran his hand over his hair. "I may not have been around him at every moment of his life, but there's no way he had— Do you know what you're asking? You're asking me if he killed children."

"What about old newspaper articles? I found a whole bunch of them inside the walls. All about missing kids."

Uncle George shook his head. "Don't know anything about them. Or why they'd be in the walls." He pointed a shaky finger at him, his face red, tears bubbling in his eyes. "How dare you think your *dad*, my *brother*, did the things you're thinking he did." He turned away from Benjamin.

"I'm sorry," he reached over to lay his hand on his uncle's shoulder, pausing, "but I had to ask," and pulled it back. He glanced around the cemetery and then looked down at his dad's grave. "I'm sorry."

Uncle George turned back, wiping his eyes with a quick swipe of his arm.

"It's okay. I'd probably ask the same thing."

In order to bring the situation to a more comfortable place, Benjamin decided to ask his initial question about the voices.

"How about voices? You ever hear voices at the farmhouse?"

George looked at him, eyebrows raised.

"You're a smart kid, Benjamin, but you've been through a lot lately. We all have. It's probably your tired brain tricking you."

"You've never heard them?"

"Afraid not."

"What about my dad? He ever say anything about hearing voices to you?"

"No." he chuckled. "If he did, he would've never told me. Things like that he would've kept to himself. Too much pride." George took a Kleenex from his pants pocket and wiped his nose. "Neither one of us believed in ghosts."

"So far I haven't seen anything. Just been hearing things."

"Has this voice been saying anything?"

"Nothing worth remembering," Benjamin said. It was a lie. How could he forget what it was saying?

"Maybe it's just your subconscious telling you something. Kinda like a waking dream," said George.

"Or nightmare."

"You tell Aisha?"

"Yeah. She blames stress."

"She's right. You should take a break. Go back home. Rest. This mess ain't going anywhere. Come back to it when you're ready."

"I could use a vacation. Hawaii. Maine," Benjamin said. "Somewhere other than here."

"My offer still stands, y'know. I'll take the old place off your hands."

"Actually…"

Benjamin stopped himself. For some reason he couldn't finish the sentence.

"Actually what?"

"Nothing," Benjamin said. "Nothing."

"Well, I best be going. I'll talk to you later." Uncle George hugged Benjamin and walked away. Over his shoulder, he said, "And don't worry about them ghosts, if that's what they are."

"I'll try."

George strolled through the cemetery without sidestepping plots; without considering those who lay beneath might not like the living playing on their yard.

"You probably heard our conversation," he said to his dad's stone. "Sorry. I just had to ask." Benjamin glanced back to see if his uncle was still walking through the graveyard, but he was gone. "I'm sure you know what's been happening at the farm. Crazy stuff, to be sure." He returned to his dad's marker. "Maybe I should see a psychologist. Or maybe a priest to cleanse the farmhouse." He chuckled and put his hands into his pants pockets. "I know I'm hearing voices. It's not my imagination playing around with me. I don't know. It's like déjà vu. Like the voices seem familiar. Like I know who they are…but I don't know who they are. Know what I mean? It's confusing, I know. I'm definitely confused."

The sound of a tractor stole his attention. He could make it out beyond his car. It was a backhoe. Its metal arm dug into the ground and deposited the earth next to it.

"Looks like you're getting a new neighbor."

At that moment, he thought about his own death. He never put much thought into it. Since his dad's passing, it surrounded him, and he didn't realize it until now.

The plots on either side of his dad's were eternal strangers. Names he didn't know. His dad lay there alone. He didn't even know where his mother was buried.

He figured when his time came, he'd choose cremation.

CHAPTER THIRTY-SIX

The next morning, Benjamin woke in his own bed with the thought of the children on his mind. He couldn't remember if he dreamt about them, but there they were waiting for him. It wasn't so much that *all* of the children were on his mind. Only two.

He sat up and rubbed his face, clearing the webs from his groggy head. He thought about his discoveries: the children's remains beneath the barn, and the articles within the wall, and Tyson... So where did that leave the two children? He or she had to be somewhere on the property. Was there another manmade cellar outside? Did another wall hold the key? And why were the two kids separated from the rest?

Downstairs, Aisha's voice called to him. "Ben, you up?"

"Coming," he hollered, standing and stretching.

Aisha sat at the kitchen table, eating a plate of eggs and bacon. "Morning."

He sat down and poured himself a glass of orange juice and stared at his plate. The eggs and bacon didn't appeal to him. He pushed it away.

"Aren't you hungry?"

"Not really."

"You feeling okay? I can make you toast if you want."

"No, thanks. Just not hungry."

With big black eyes, Hogarth sat next to him and laid his chin on his thigh. "Pouring it on, don't you think?" He grabbed a strip of bacon from his plate and the dog shot into a stance. "Here you go." He tossed it into the air, and Hogarth snatched it with his mouth.

"How you feeling this morning?" Benjamin said.

"Huh?"

"How are you feeling?"

"Oh, okay, I guess. Think I got a bug or something." Aisha wiped her mouth with a napkin.

"Maybe you should lie down."

"I'm fine."

She pushed some scrambled eggs around on her plate with her fork. "Seems like Detective Lane has his ducks in order. Pretty positive they got their guy. With all those pictures this creep had, I'd have to agree."

"Me too."Benjamin grabbed a piece of bacon and took a small bite. "There's one thing that has been bothering me. Woke up this morning thinking about it."

"What's that?"

"There's still two children missing. We have twenty-two articles, but only had nineteen bodies in the barn cellar. Where're the other two children?"

Aisha sipped her orange juice.

"I wonder where Darren…" She pushed her plate away, sniffling.

"Me too," Benjamin said.

He reached over the table, and she grabbed his hand.

"We'll get him back," he said. "We will. I'm sure of it."

Aisha gave him a small smile. He knew it was the best she could give under the circumstances. She was being brave, and he smiled back. Silence fell between them for a moment, and then Aisha asked, "You think the two kids are in this house somewhere? Maybe outside?"

"Not sure, but I think we should search this damned house first. Knock on walls, rip up carpet, whatever's needed, starting with my dad's room."

???

The morning sunlight revealed the dirty room.

"We gotta move this old bed out into the hall," Benjamin said. "Clear some of this trash. I wanna see this room plain. We'll have to clear out *all* the rooms. I don't want to miss anything."

Once the room was clear, he scanned the ragged carpet for anything out of the ordinary. If it was torn, or if a piece had been replaced. Something that would be a clue to a secret.

"Do you think the carpet is original?" she said.

"Looks like it. Seems intact. Hasn't been pulled away anywhere. No discolored sections. I don't think my dad would've spent money where he didn't have to."

She turned to face Ben. "But he built that wall you tore down."

"He probably hired someone to build it. At his age, I'm not sure if he could've done it alone."

"And the articles?"

"Look, whoever helped him had to have put them there. My dad probably didn't even know they were there." He walked over and glanced out the window. "I used to think my dad was an ox, you know that, but after coming here, seeing how he lived, I think he needed a lot of help, especially from me." He stepped back over to her. "Whoever helped him build that wall took advantage of an old man."

"You think he'd give the walls a second coat of paint? Or no, because he'd want to save the money?"

"Probably not. Why?"

She pointed. "Down there, in the sunlight, it looks like there's a small section that has been repainted."

"Where?" Benjamin walked over to the wall.

"Near the corner, down low."

He knelt and rubbed his hand over the spot. "Yeah, I can see it."

"You think there are more articles in the wall?"

"Don't know. Maybe." Benjamin stood up. "But we're going to find out."

???

After a few punches into the wall with a sledgehammer, Benjamin and Aisha were able to peer inside. Three shoeboxes sat stacked on top of one another. They glanced at each other for a brief moment; then Benjamin pulled one out at a time. They were covered in bits of drywall and dust.

"I want to look, but I don't want to look," Aisha said.

"I know how you feel."

They were both kneeling toward each other, the three boxes spread out side by side between them.

Benjamin took in a deep breath and released a long sigh. "Well…"

He lifted its lid, and inside lay Polaroids. They both reached in and glanced through a few.

Benjamin quickly replaced the lid and stared at Aisha. His stomach kicked acid up into his throat. He wanted to vomit, but held back the urge by swallowing the burning liquid down.

Aisha's face was in shock. The whites of her brown eyes large and revealing, tears brimming, her mouth slacked.

For a minute, neither he nor she said anything. They couldn't say anything. The pictures said it for them.

He closed his eyes. "Please tell me that's not what I think it is."

"Oh my god," she said. "They're…naked and…"

Benjamin broke down and sobbed. "I can't believe it. I just can't. Why would...? He's not..." He took in a couple of deep breaths and clenched his hands into fists. "He's a monster. A goddamned monster!"

"We gotta call Detective Lane," she said.

Ben wiped his face with his hands. "Yeah, I know, it's just..."

"I know."

"Do you? Do you really know?" he said. "Do you understand what this says?" She reached over to him, and he swept her hand away. "No. I want you to tell me what you know!"

"I know we have to call the cops," Aisha said.

"No! What do *you* know?"

"I don't know!" she said, standing. "All I know is my son is missing. *That's* what I know."

Benjamin hung his head and sighed. "And all I know is that my dad was a child molester and killer."

After a moment of silence, Aisha said, "Do you think the other boxes have pictures too?"

"Probably." After a heavy sigh, he grabbed her hand. "Not sure if I wanna look."

"Don't you think we have to?"

"Have to? Yeah. Want to? Hell no."

"We have to," she said. "Maybe these will help us find Darren. Those..." she pointed at the boxes, "those could be Darren."

All three boxes contained pictures of children. The photographer of the pictures was unknown, but the bedroom where these pictures were taken in was. So was the bed.

They cried as they skimmed through them, horror and disgust smeared across their faces like the blood on those in the photographs.

The lids were replaced onto the shoeboxes. Silence choked the room. Tears flowed from their eyes.

"They're of the same children in the articles," Aisha said, wiping her eyes.

"I know," he said.

"We have to match these photos to the articles."

Benjamin arched his brows. "Are you kidding me? I can't look at them long enough to do that. We have to call Detective Lane. The sheriff!"

"We have to," she said. "Whoever is left unmatched could leave us with the two missing kids."

"Do you really want to look through those?" Benjamin stood and picked up the sledgehammer from the floor. "I know I don't."

"I don't want to either, but it's the only way."

"We have to call Detective Lane," he said.

"I wanna know." Aisha grabbed the three shoeboxes. "I have to know."

???

Downstairs, Aisha fought back her emotions as she matched photo to article. It wasn't an easy task for obvious reasons. The photos in the articles were of happy, normal children compared to their terror-stricken counterparts.

A crash came from upstairs, followed by Benjamin screaming. Aisha dropped the pictures and ran up the staircase with Hogarth on her heels. When she came to the bedroom door, Benjamin was smashing holes into the walls with the sledgehammer.

"Fuck!" he bellowed. "You fucking sick fuck!"

Aisha could only watch as he released his anger.

"I'm glad you hung yourself!"

He swung the sledgehammer into the wall, pulled it out, and swung again. Drywall exploded into the air, a billow of dust followed. He repeated it over and over until he stopped and fell to his knees, releasing the hammer. Sweat covered his reddened face, his breathing quick and hard.

Aisha couldn't understand what he was feeling. Couldn't even pretend to know. Discovering your dad was someone or something different than what you grew up knowing was not only shocking but heartbreaking.

Benjamin loved his dad. He loved the old man who worked the fields with his bare hands, had silly adages, collected baseball cards, and raised him to be the man he was today. How do you sort the emotions that run wild through your mind, your heart? How do you make sense of everything you thought you knew about the only person you loved? Was his dad's love for him a lie? Who *was* his dad?

???

Aisha called Detective Lane and explained what they found. In no time, he was at the farm with Detective Haines and Sheriff Tucker.

"Apparently we can't do our job," said the sheriff. "Is there anything else you should tell us? You see Bigfoot? Little green men come and probe ya? In all of my life, I never—"

"That's enough, Sheriff," said Detective Lane.

"That's everything," Benjamin said, putting his arm around Aisha.

"The both of you are heading back to Pittsburgh immediately. We're going to comb the entire property from the bottom up. Every acre, inch by inch." Detective Lane looked at the sheriff. "*Again.*" Then back to Benjamin and Aisha, "There's been a lot discovered here, and there's probably more here somewhere."

"Consider us gone," Aisha said.

CHAPTER THIRTY-SEVEN

With Aisha and Hogarth at her place, Benjamin took simple pleasure in sleeping in his big bed for a change, showering in his own bathroom, and eating in his own kitchen. He almost felt relieved.

For the first time in a long time, he thought about his novel. The one he was supposed to have spent the summer writing. His original idea didn't excite him anymore. Instead, he thought he should change it up and write about the current hell he and Aisha endured. A nonfiction book. *I'm a journalist after all, aren't I?* It made sense to use his skills in such an undertaking. It seemed his job wasn't such a burden on him any longer. But it would have to wait.

The sun began setting and turned the blue sky into an azure canvas with a sprinkling of glitter high above. He decided to take a walk toward town and enjoy the crisp night. As Benjamin passed beneath some maple trees, his cell phone pulled him away from the warm evening. He checked the caller ID and answered it.

"Hello, Detective."

"Hello, Mr. Cole."

Benjamin stopped on the sidewalk. "How can I help you?"

"I assure you it's not—"

"So, no word on Darren then?" Benjamin said.

"No," said Detective Lane. "I'm afraid not." A moment of silence passed. "I'm sorry I can't be there to speak to you in person, but I'm calling because I wanted to tell you that our suspect, Eugene Greely, isn't our man."

"What? Are you fucking kidding me? Why? You said he was!"

"I know. But he's been released and cleared on all charges. He will be receiving some therapy with his fascination for photographing children. It turns out he is just a simple man who likes to take pictures."

"He's still sick," Benjamin said.

"That's why he'll be getting help. Raised in orphanages until he was eighteen. Never had a childhood. At least not the one he wished he had. So he took photographs of children living out what he didn't have. Things like that. Kid things. He lived through his photos. Nothing more."

"Jesus Christ, Aisha's going to freak out when I tell her."

A brief moment of silence.

"Another thing… Your dad…he was a big baseball card collector, wasn't he?" said Detective Lane.

"Yeah, he had boxes full of them."

"You ever look in those boxes, Mister Cole?"

"No. Never got around to it once we found the shoeboxes in the wall."

"What we found in those boxes were more Polaroids of those children in the articles. They were mixed in with the cards. Except, these ones were far more disturbing than the ones you found in the wall. These photos also had your dad in them *with* the children. Doing things…"

The sidewalk tilted. Benjamin couldn't believe what he was hearing. The world had already crashed on him, but this news swept the ground out beneath him, making him fall further into his own personal hell. "Jesus Christ." He sat on the ground, his knees bent, and rested his head in his hand. "Why…why would that sick *fucker* have those photos lying around in a box in his collector's room? The other ones were hidden in the wall. Doesn't make sense."

"As far as I can guess—and as you just stated—that was his collector's room. It appears your dad collected more than baseball cards. Sometimes hiding things in plain sight is the best way to hide things. Hell, we should've looked in those boxes the last time we swept the area, but *we* or the sheriff didn't. We were too focused on the outside of the house. But I really don't know. Maybe the ones in the wall were taken first. Or he considered them more special. Just guessing, really. But it wasn't just one baseball card box full. It was all of them."

"All?"

"I'm afraid so."

"Every box?" Benjamin slammed his fist into the grass.

Both the articles and the images of the children in the shoeboxes he and Aisha found ran through Benjamin's mind. He couldn't keep them straight or control them from coming and going. Like flashes of lightning sprung loose on a summer's evening without a cloud to manage it.

"I laid a lot on you, and trust me, that's not my intention. You've been through a lot. I just thought you needed to know."

"Now I know why my…that so-called human being hung himself." Benjamin stood. "Fucking animal couldn't face who he was."

"That was one thing I wondered about when I first read over all the information regarding the farm. Why did someone at his age commit suicide? Now we know."

Benjamin closed his cell and felt sick. With all the bad news and discoveries, the latest info was hard to swallow, but it could have been worse. The detective could've been calling with horrible news about Darren.

CHAPTER THIRTY-EIGHT

After his call to Aisha, Benjamin lay on the couch and dozed in and out of sleep. The only light in the house was the glow emanating from the television screen. On TV, raucous laughter came from an unseen crowd.

The laughter slid its way into Benjamin's ears and into sleep.

Darkness.

He couldn't see, but he could hear the laughing of children from all around him. It sounded guttural, almost painful. He reached out with his hand and felt a string. The air was cool and damp. He could smell the earth, its bitter stench filling his nostrils like packed mud.

The laughter morphed into garbles, and then into screams.

Don't pull the string.

He grabbed it.

Don't.

He pulled the cord.

After his eyes adjusted to the bright light, he found himself standing in the grave that was built beneath the barn. A mirror stood before him. In it, he saw his own reflection. It was pale, featureless.

Benjamin touched his face. Even though his reflection had no eyes, he saw himself. The children's screams echoed from behind him. In the mirror he saw nothing, only himself and the muddied room. He turned around. Sitting on the earthen floor were all of the children from the articles who were murdered, raped, abused, and who called this place home for so long.

He stepped back and his foot sank into the mud. He tried to yank it out but his other foot got stuck as well. His whole body started to sink.

Help!

He reached above to grab at the pull string, but it danced at his fingertips, just out of his reach.

All of the children stood and came toward him with their arms outward. Their faces were battered and bloodied. Black and blue marks smeared across their young skin. Years of tears carved streaks from their eyes on down through their cheeks like a raging river tearing away at sediment.

Help me!

A young girl of about eight leaned into him and said, "Please. Help. Help me."

Her breath smelled like spoiled milk. Her flesh like decayed roadkill.

Benjamin was waist-high now. He tried to scream, but he had no mouth.

Bones cracked as the girl reached over and cupped a hand over where his mouth would have been. Its smell made Benjamin gag. Like the fresh kill of a deer hanging in a barn with its guts dangling out. It smelled like death. With her other hand on top of his head, she pushed him down, joints popping as she did so.

NO!

Then they all screamed.

And as they did, it turned into a single low, deep chuckle.

Benjamin snapped open his eyes when he realized the chuckle came at his ear. Warm and heavy. A gloved hand clamped over his mouth and squeezed. Before his eyes could adjust, a voice said, "We're taking a ride."

A sudden explosion of pain rattled Benjamin's head.

Stars bloomed.

Then darkness.

CHAPTER THIRTY-NINE

Holland, New York. December 20, 1970.

Heavy flakes fell, partially obscuring Michael's view of the evergreen trees. Their scent wafted through the cold, night air. Christmas lights decorated a small shack bustling with customers. A boy or girl laughed. A man bellowed, "Ho, Ho, Ho." Someone else whistled a Christmas song. Michael hunched his shoulders, buttoned his wool coat, and blew into his hands to warm them as wet snow peppered his face. He knocked on the driver's window of the idling VW Beetle. Seconds later, it rolled down and revealed Betty's thin face, her eyes squinting against the snow coming into the car.

"The faster you go get one, the faster we can get home." In her arms, and bundled in blankets, she held their sleeping infant.

"I'm actually surprised there's so many left, being so close to Christmas," he said.

She adjusted the blanket around the baby. "That's what I'm letting the heat out for?"

"Funny. You guys stay nice and warm while I fight the elements to get our family a tree."

"We'll be here waiting."

"Well, don't let me keep you from your comfy abode. I shall return with our first family Christmas tree. Oh, and you're tying it to the hood." He winked at her and started kicking through the snow-covered lot toward the trees.

Over his shoulder he heard her say, "You're such a Scrooge, Michael," followed by laughter.

He passed two men who were shoving a tree into the back of a Ford Bronco and thought how cold they would be on their way home.

"Braver than me," he said.

The light from the strands of bulbs that hung above helped Michael's vision as he walked down a row where taller and wider trees stood like soldiers, unmoving. He cut between two and stopped when a boy ran by, yelling after someone ahead of him. He stepped out into the row. The trees in front of him were much smaller. Maybe six feet. Not too big for his car to carry.

"Ah, Douglas firs. Good choice," said a voice from behind him. "We got them in last week. You like it?"

Michael turned. "Oh. Uh… You didn't grow it here at the tree farm?"

"Nope. These ones were shipped in from the West Coast. So you like it? I can twine her up and tie it to the hood of your Beetle."

"How much?" said Michael.

"How much you got?" said the man.

"What?"

"Just kidding you. Trees in this row, these smaller ones," he pointed, "are fifteen. If you want one of the bigger ones, then that'll cost—"

"Wait. How did you know I drove a Beetle?"

"I saw you talking to your wife in it."

"Not yet. We're getting married in the spring."

The man held his hands up. "My mistake."

"It's all right. She gets to sit in the warm car with my son while I'm out here freezing my butt off."

"Son? How old?"

"Just a little guy. Newborn. Not even a month old yet."

"What's the little fella's name?" said the man.

"Ben."

"Not very fatherly of you to drag him out here in the snow, don't you think?"

Michael chuckled.

"My fiancée wanted to do this as a family. First Christmas and all."

"Gotcha," said the man. "Now, how about this tree?"

Michael looked it over. "Yeah, I think this will be the one."

"Good." A smile crept on the man's face. "I'll go get some twine to tie her up with." He gave Michael a wink. "Stay here and admire your family's first Christmas tree."

"Okay, thanks."

As the man walked away, Michael hollered, "Merry Christmas."

"Merry Christmas," said the man without looking back.

Michael ran his hand over the snow-covered branches and watched the powder fall to his boots. He plucked a needle, crushed it, and smelled it. Its sweet fragrance caused him to release a small laugh.

"What's so funny, mister?"

Next to Michael, a young boy of about ten stared up at him.

He let go of the tree needle and wiped his hand on his pant leg. "Nothing."

"You always laugh at nothing?" The boy didn't break his stare.

"Shouldn't you be with your parents?"

From somewhere in the midst of all the trees and people, a woman screamed, "Billy!"

Michael glanced around for the woman. He turned back and the boy still remained, staring at him.

"That's my mom," he said.

"Billy!" the woman cried again.

"I should go."

Michael didn't say a word as the boy ran off down the aisle and disappeared between two trees.

In the distance, the woman's voice berated the boy. "I told you to stay by my side, didn't I? Huh? Didn't I? Wait until your father hears about this."

Coming toward him, an older man in a sweatshirt, gloves, and a winter cap with a small cloth apron around his waist said, "Can I help you with a tree?"

"I've been helped, thank you."

The worker continued on and spoke to another man and his teenage daughter.

When Michael got to the shack, only a handful of customers were paying for their trees. He glanced at the people around him and didn't see the man who helped him earlier. A woman wearing the same small apron around her waist walked past.

"Excuse me? I'm looking for an employee. He said he was getting twine for the tree I picked out. I can't seem to find him."

"Was he an older man?"

"No. Younger. Late thirties, maybe."

"Was he tall, lanky?" said the woman.

"No. A little taller than myself. Six feet, I guess."

"Was he wearing one of these aprons?" She grabbed her own and let it fall back.

Michael sighed out of frustration. "He was just a man who was helping me."

"Then he doesn't work here. There are only three of us here tonight. Our other two helpers called in sick."

Michael thought for a moment. He didn't know what to make of it.

"I'm helping customers, but if you can wait a moment I can help you next, okay?"

"Sure," said Michael.

She walked away, calling after a couple, "I can ring you up now if you'd like."

Michael hoped Betty and his new pride and joy, Ben, were nice and cozy. He'd filled the Beetle's tank before they left home, so they should be fine.

Large flakes continued to fall as he peered out into the parking lot. Only a handful of cars remained. A van with a large tree tied to its top turned onto the main road. At the far end of the lot, two trucks were parked, blanketed in what looked like a sheet of cotton. Beyond them, an oldie of a wagon sat by itself. It didn't wear the same coat of snow the others wore. It was wiped clean, the whole thing. It looked out of place.

Michael looked over to where he left Betty and his son. Where he left his family.

The VW Beetle was gone.

He trudged through the snow and glanced around the lot. His stomach knotted, heart thudded in his throat. *Where did they go?*

The couple the woman employee helped earlier was brushing off the windows of their rumbling truck. White plumes of smoke coughed from its tailpipe. He ran over to them. A large tree lay in its bed. The woman climbed into the cab.

"Ex-excuse me. Did you see a VW Beetle drive off?" He pointed. "It was sitting right over there."

The man stopped brushing snow off the hood and said, "Sorry, bud. I didn't see it."

"Could I get a lift into town?" He put his hands into his pockets. "My car's gone."

"Stolen?" said the man.

"I don't think so. I was looking to buy a tree. And when I came out, it was gone. My fiancée and my son were waiting inside it. I can pay you. I think I got thirty bucks in my wallet."

The man stared at him, and then rubbed the back of his hand against his beard, as if thinking about Michael's offer.

"I promise. I'm not some murderer or kidnapper. I'm just worried is all."

The frosted driver's side window rolled down, and the woman said, "It's Christmas, Bill. We have room to give him a ride into town. We're going that way anyway." She looked over at Michael. "And we don't need your money."

"Go ahead," said the man. "Get in."

Michael ran around to the other side and hopped in.

The man tossed his brush into the bed of the truck and climbed in. "You're right, honey," he said, rolling up the window. "You're always right."

"I know," she said.

The truck jolted into gear and grumbled as the driver turned it around. Without signaling, they turned onto the main road and puttered toward town.

Through the back window of the truck, Michael studied the tree farm. Why would she leave? Was she mad because he took too long? Even if Betty were mad, she wouldn't have left him there.

His gaze fell to the old wagon in the lot.

Would she?

CHAPTER FORTY

Two things were evident when Benjamin woke up: the pulsing ache on the side of his head and the pitch-black of the room. He touched above his ear and groaned at its tenderness. A patch of his hair was clumped together. *Blood.* He rolled onto his side and pushed himself into a sitting position. His hands came away with dirt, and he wiped them on his pants. The damp air clung to him. The room was cool. He took in a breath and let the familiar smell of earth fill him with an image of where he was. *The barn cellar.*

By now, he knew the room quite well, intimately. It gave him the bodies of children. It offered him Tyson. It revealed itself to him. He and the cellar had a bond. A dark and sick one. The grave wasn't just a hole, a dumping ground for the dead, it was the beginning. It was his roots. The day his old man took the tractor and dug out the pit, it birthed nightmares. It gave life to Benjamin. It was the beginning of a new family tree. It was his past, and it was his future. It was his dad.

His thoughts ran to the last moment he remembered before waking up to his current surroundings, but he couldn't recall who or what brought him to the cellar.

With a grunt, he stood and held out his arms for balance. Pain squeezed his head like a boa constricting a rabbit, and he stumbled to the side trying to gain his sea legs. His hand pressed against the soft wall, and he took a moment to gather himself. After a few deep sighs, he reached into the air and waved his arm back and forth. It was here. The pull string. He turned and took a few steps forward and then felt it slide over his wrist. He wrestled for it, and once he gripped it, he closed his eyes and pulled.

One thing Benjamin learned from the previous times he'd found himself in the cellar and tugged on the pull string was that it would explode with light. He shielded his face with his hands and when he opened them—

—the cellar presented another body.

Benjamin startled, but he didn't scurry back in horror or clamber up the ladder out of fear like the past two times. In a small way, he had become desensitized to the deceased. The dead had become the norm. He shook his head, clenched his hand, and punched the wall. A clump of dirt fell away.

"Damn it!" He turned and faced the body that was propped up in the corner. "Looks like Bradford just dwindled by one. Huh, Sheriff?"

Benjamin stepped forward and leaned in toward Sheriff Tucker's body. He was sitting up, his uniform dirty but together. His hat atop his bulbous head. The sheriff's eyes were open; a perpetual stare. Their whites filled red. His chubby mouth was slack, tube-like lips pale. His face was splattered with what reminded Benjamin of measles. Red spots about the chin and cheeks. No longer did his face wear a sour look as it did when he first came to the house. It was relaxed. The collar of his shirt wore a dark stain. His neck possessed a thick, black smile from one side to the other.

Benjamin spun away, gagging.

A wave of heat wrapped around him. Sweat bubbled up on his forehead. He closed his eyes and thought of something breezy and refreshing. A swim in the ocean. A cold beer. A crisp autumn day. Anything else. He was sure he'd vomit whatever his stomach could produce.

He wiped his forehead with his hand and saw the foot of the ladder in front of him. He took a deep breath and exhaled. At the bottom of the ladder, he took another breath and climbed. At the top, he pushed against the trapdoor, but it didn't budge. With his head lowered and his back arched, he lunged upward and slammed into it. He pushed. His leg muscles tightened. He grunted and gritted his teeth, eyes clenched.

Crack!

He released his effort and took a moment to catch his breath. His back stung with pain. His head pulsed.

Although the rung he stood on held his weight, it had a split. He lowered himself back down to the tomb and dug into his pants pockets. Nothing but lint.

The room felt smaller, as if the walls had closed in on him. He wasn't used to enclosed spaces, especially ones that could end up being his own grave. His breathing sped up. *Calm down.* He took a moment to gather himself. *Just breathe.* Benjamin considered the scene before him.

Sheriff.

As if a skunk had sprayed the dead man, Benjamin scrunched his nose, held his breath, and pulled the sheriff toward the center of the room by his ankles. The man's body trudged outward, little by little. His hat fell off. Benjamin strained to get the large man into position. After a short rest, he pulled again and again until he dropped his legs and knelt beside him.

Since he was much closer to Sheriff Tucker, the smell of death permeated his nose. It smelled of burnt hair and bad breath. The bad breath that smacked you in the morning when someone yawned in your face. From someone who slept with their mouth open all night, catching flies and spiders.

He searched the front pockets of the sheriff's pants and found nothing. He leaned into him and shoved until the man rolled onto his side. He felt the big man's back pockets. Nothing. The body fell back. Benjamin patted the sheriff's shirt pockets and came away with a receipt from Linda's Flower Shack. Whoever killed him had done their part and cleaned him out except for the piece of paper.

The sheriff paid cash for a half a dozen Gerber daisies. Benjamin glanced at the man's large hand. No wedding band. He thought back to the times he spoke to the sheriff and tried to remember if he had noticed one or not. Didn't matter. From his years of interviewing police officers back in Pittsburgh, he knew that a lot of them didn't wear their rings for safety reasons. In case it got caught in something or interfered with their weapon. It was practical and nothing more.

Married or not, the sheriff loved someone. Someone loved him.

"Gerber daisies. Can't recall the last time I bought flowers for Aisha. Have I ever?"

Aisha?

Did she know he was gone? How long had he been down here?

I need to get out of here.

Benjamin crumpled the paper and tossed it toward the sheriff's upside down hat. He missed. Something inside it caught his attention. He grabbed it up, reached in, and pulled out several items. A silver dollar. A can of Skoal. And the lock knife. "Couldn't have left the candy bar?" Benjamin placed the other items inside the sheriff's shirt pocket, flipped open the knife, and took to the ladder.

Benjamin gripped the knife so its blade faced outward, as if he were about to chip away at a block of ice. He stepped down a rung to give himself room, and after several run-throughs of how he was going to go at it, he decided the good old-fashioned stabbing arc that Norman Bates' mother used to slash away at Marion during the shower scene in *Psycho* would be best, even though it would be awkward. It would be noisy, but there was no way around it.

He stabbed the underside of the trapdoor, and with the knife's tip dug in, he pushed to the side so the knife would act like a lever and pry the wood away. Only a small piece splintered. He pulled away and hit it again. Then again. And again. Each blow followed by the levering of wood away. He worked at the same spot over and over. When he first found the door, he used cutters to bust its lock. What was in its place, he could only guess.

He took a breather. Sweat streaked down his face. The room no longer felt cool; instead, it felt muggy. He wiped bits of wood and dust from his face. Where the knife punched the trapdoor, a decent-sized hole remained. Benjamin swung the knife as best he could and slammed it into the hole he created. The knife stuck in a good half-inch. He leaned his weight into the ladder, letting go of the knife, and rubbed the back of his neck. *Can't stop now.* Gripping the knife with his left hand, he hammered its butt with his right palm. Another hit. Then again. Each one dug the blade deeper. Again.

With both hands he wiggled it back and forth until it loosened from the wood. He needed to copy his actions next to the hole. Do it all over again. Dig, or chip away at the door, and then hammer away at the end of the knife. Once it punched through, it would make the hole larger. After several more attacks, he could reach a hand through, maybe his entire arm, and feel for the lock.

It took a while. How long, he didn't know. An hour? Two? Sweat soaked through his shirt. He pulled chips of wood from his hair and licked the dust from his lips and spat. The palm of his hand throbbed with pain, sore to the touch. He stretched his fingers to ease their stiffness. Benjamin wished the hatch had been made from two by fours. It would have made for an easier escape, but the door was made from a solid piece of wood, and not plywood either.

He folded the knife, put it into his pocket, and put his face to the hole. The air was crisp. Crickets chirped from somewhere.

Benjamin reached through the hole with ease. He felt around and grasped a long, thick metal bar. He glided his hand over it, then back the other way, and paused where it went through the padlock loop. He pushed it back through the ring and pulled his arm inside. He put his hands against the trapdoor and pushed. The door opened, fell back to the floor, and he climbed out.

Stretching out on his back, he took in the night air. He sat up and scanned the house for movement through the barn entrance. As he sat there, staring at it, Benjamin no longer saw the house before him but instead saw the memory of it, of him playing by the old oak tree with his Matchbox cars.

In the setting sun, his younger self dug a hole beneath a root and used it as a hideaway for his Gran Torino while his police car smashed into the trunk of the tree. "You'll never get me, copper!" He made the sound of squealing tires and steered the Torino off around a rock.

A Safari wagon pulling up next to his dad's truck grabbed his attention. A hand waved from inside it. Young Benjamin waved back. And just as its engine died, his dad yelled out from the barn's entrance.

"Ben. I want you to get in the house. Go ahead. It's getting late."

As he gathered his cars and headed toward the house, the driver's side door of the old car opened. When he grabbed the screen door to enter, a voice rang out.

"Get in the back seat!"

Ben turned to his Uncle George swatting at a little girl who screamed from the front seat.

His dad came running over and pointed at Ben. "I told you to get in the house!"

He didn't move. He watched his uncle grab at the girl, who kicked back. The next moment, the passenger side door flung open, and she came around and ran straight for him.

It happened fast. Too fast.

Ben dropped his cars and stood frozen. He didn't react as it happened. She came toward him, her face filled with tears and terror. His uncle slamming his door with anger in his eyes. His dad with arms wide open and a look of shock on his face as he ran toward him. Was it shock? Was it fear? Fear for Ben? Or fear that he and Uncle George were found out?

No. It happened in slow motion. Too slow.

He remembered the voice. Her voice.

"Please! Please help!" She grabbed him by the arms. "Help me!"

Uncle George grabbed her from behind and lifted her off the ground and carried her to the barn. She flailed her arms and legs and screamed.

Ben's dad gripped him by the shoulders, kneeling before him, and said, "That little girl did something bad, Ben. You don't say nothing about this, hear me?"

Ben nodded as he watched her and Uncle George disappear into the barn.

"Look at me. You keep your mouth shut, hear me? It's our secret. Forever and ever."

Benjamin shook himself from the reverie. His eyes wet from tears he had no idea he had shed until now. He wiped them away. "Oh my god!"

It made sense to him now. The girl's voice. It was *her* voice. Not stress or anxiety, or a ghost, but an actual girl's voice. His heart thudded against his chest, and then lodged itself in his throat. He shivered at the thought, and the hairs on his arms rose.

It's our secret. Forever and ever.

"Dad!"

He stood and kicked an old coffee can. Nails flew across the barn.

Uncle George!

He leaned against the workbench, balled his fists, and fought back more tears that welled up. His heart raced. He wanted to destroy his dad, his uncle. He picked up a hammer, then tossed it to the side. It slid and stopped next to the trapdoor.

The sheriff.

Tyson.

The children.

That girl.

Benjamin spotted a gas can in the corner and picked it up. He shook it, and it swished with liquid. He removed the cap and gave it a sniff. The strong smell of gasoline assaulted his nose. After he replaced the lid, he searched the many jars and tin cans that littered the workbench. A few minutes later, he found what he was looking for in a beaten-up cigar box.

Matches.

CHAPTER FORTY-ONE

As Aisha raced over to Benjamin's house, she made a phone call to Detective Lane and left him a message. In her hand, she held the letter. It simply read, *Want To See Both Of Your Boys Alive? Come To The Farmhouse ALONE!*

She left her car running and ran onto the porch. "No. No. No." And banged on the front door. "Benjamin!" She rang the doorbell several times. "Benjamin! You in there?"

She went back to her car, cut the engine, and rummaged through her keys to find Benjamin's house key. Before she could get back to the door, her cell rang. Detective Lane's name appeared on the screen.

"Oh, thank god, it's you," she said. "They got Benjamin!"

"What? Where are you?"

"At his house."

"Are you sure?" said the detective.

"I got another letter. It says to go to the farm alone if I want to see *both* of my boys alive. Darren is still alive." Her body trembled and she began to cry. "I've called Benjamin's cell, pounded on his door. No answer. I have to go to the farm."

"No. Don't do that. Listen to me. I want you to meet me at the Oakmont station."

"They want me to come alone. If I don't, then—"

"I can't let you go there alone. I *need* you to go straight to the station, okay? Remember back at the hotel you made me promise that I'd get Darren back? Remember? Now I need you to make me a promise."

"All right, I'll be there. Promise."

???

Detective Lane handed her a cup of coffee and sat across from her in a metal folding chair. "It's not Starbucks, but it's what we got."

Aisha set it on the desk next to her. "So what are we going to do?"

"*We* won't be doing anything. I'll be doing something," he said. "It's far too dangerous to have you there. Besides, if something happened to you, it'd be my ass on the line."

Aisha bolted up from her chair. "They instructed for *me* to go there!"

"Please, Ms. Jones. Please sit." The detective stared at her. "Please."

She sat down and took a sip of her coffee.

"I had you come here for safety reasons. This could be a set-up. Probably is. They already grabbed your son, and now they grabbed Benjamin. We can't take the chance they'd go for the trifecta."

"I don't care, I'm going with you."

"I can't allow it."

"Then I'm heading home." She set her cup on the desk. "You have no need for me here, and you can't detain me."

"You're right, I can't. But I highly suggest you stay here. We can put you up in a motel."

She secured her purse over her shoulder. "I'm going home."

Detective Lane grasped her arm and led her outside.

"Look, my ass will be on the line if I take you with me. That is a surefire way to get me fired. Or you killed. Or both. I won't do that."

"Then thank you for wasting my time, Benjamin's time, and more importantly, Darren's time, because right now Benjamin and my son could be dead. I can take care of myself."

Aisha climbed into her car and sped off.

CHAPTER FORTY-TWO

Aisha didn't head home. Instead, she sped through the night to the farmhouse. The pregnant moon illuminated the woods as she parked her car against them and cut the engine. She walked along the shadows to conceal herself. It only gave coverage for a few hundred feet before she would have to run across Coal Run Road to the wooden fence that surrounded the farm. She would follow it along the drive to keep her in view of the house.

When she came to the end of the woods, where she would have to sprint across the dirt road, a hand grabbed her by the shoulder.

Aisha started and turned around to Detective Lane.

"You scared the shit out of me."

"Shhh. Did you really think that I thought you were going home?" he whispered. "You know I can arrest you and stick you in my car down the road?"

"You could," she whispered back. "Yeah."

Detective Lane thought for a moment. "You stick close to me, and what I say is gospel, got it?"

"They're expecting *me*. I'm supposed to show up *alone*, remember?"

He stroked his hair back. "Yeah, I know."

"Did you bring back-up?" she whispered.

"I got two guys. They'll go on my call."

She held up her fingers. "Two? You kidding me? Shouldn't the whole force be here?"

"You seem to forget this is Bradford. Manpower is beyond limited, so I brought Detective Haines and Deputy Rudnick."

Aisha held her hands out before her in disbelief. "Holy— Then call other departments from nearby towns."

"The deputy assures me they're on their way, but since they're miles away, it'll take some time."

"What about the sheriff? Where's he at?"

"Not sure. Deputy said he couldn't reach him."

"Could've brought more boys from Oakmont," she said.

Detective Lane sighed and ignored her as he pulled a small walkie-talkie from his hip and clicked it. "Carl. Come in." He let go of the button and said, "We're all we got."

Detective Haines' voice came over the handset. "Go ahead."

"You guys set?" said Detective Lane.

"Just say when."

"Good."

"Remember," said Detective Haines. "Just act. You wanted New York, remember? Here's your chance."

"What's that all about?" whispered Aisha.

"Nothing," he said. "Look. Detective Haines, the deputy, and I will be the sleight of hand. You play your part by walking in through the front door."

"How do you know they just won't shoot me?"

"They won't. Not after all the work they put into this."

"Do I at least get a gun?"

"Can't do that."

She arched her brows. "Figures."

The detective stared at her for a moment, took in a deep breath, released it, and then raised his walkie and clicked the button. "Carl?"

"Here."

"Start flanking the west side of the farmhouse, I'll meet you around back. Stay in the shadows and keep your eyes focused. Keep this line squeaky clean. I'll check your location when needed. And stay safe. Over and out."

Detective Lane turned the volume down to zero on his handset and returned it to its holster.

Aisha chewed her bottom lip.

"Ready?" said Detective Lane.

"An hour ago."

"Just hug the fence line until you get to the house. And try to keep calm. I know it's not easy, but try. Just walk through the front door just like they requested. Detective Haines and I will be close by. Any questions?"

"Will there be donuts afterward?"

CHAPTER FORTY-THREE

The moonlight cast long shadows across the dirt driveway as Aisha walked along the wooden fence toward the house. Its windows appeared black, stark against the old place. Eyeless sockets in a pale skull. As she opened the screen door, its hinges creaked. She grasped the doorknob of the front door and began to turn it—

Bang!

Her breath hitched in her throat. She grabbed her chest. Aisha turned toward the barn and waited for a moment. She turned back to the house and eased its door open. She entered and disappeared inside as if it swallowed her whole.

Once her eyes adjusted to the darkness, the inside looked different. Dead. When she, Benjamin, and Darren slept here, it was full of life, but now it felt cold. She took careful steps and kept alert of her surroundings. The living room had been rummaged through and left in disarray. In the kitchen, cabinets were open. Dishware lay scattered on the floor, shattered. She moved aside the makeshift curtain and the basement door was half-open.

She swallowed and stole a peek around the door. Nothing. No one. At least she thought she saw no one. The darkness continued to obscure her vision. Her stomach turned.

Aisha stepped around the door. A soft sound came from down…there. She held her breath and listened. Sounded like breathing. A sort of wheezing. Short, quick panting. *Darren!* She released her breath and wiped her forehead with her arm. She hesitated to enter. Afraid to find Darren and Benjamin…dead.

"Hello?"

She stepped onto the stairs and inched her way down. The pungent smell of mold stung her eyes. Aisha guided herself by feeling along the rough wall that gave her the impression that it was made out of stones.

"I-I got your note…about coming a-alone."

Another step.

The darkness closed in around her.

Another step.

Unlike the other rooms in the house, the basement didn't have the moonlight to expose its layout. This was her first time in the basement, and at that moment, she wished it was her hundredth because she wouldn't need light to make her way.

Another step.

"Hello?"

She blinked several times to get used to the dark, but the basement didn't give in. It was pitch black.

Another step.

Another—

A hand grabbed her ankle, and Aisha tumbled headlong down the stairs.

CHAPTER FORTY-FOUR

Behind the farmhouse, Detective Lane knelt beside a small cellar window. He peered through but couldn't see anything. It was too dark. He grabbed his walkie and turned its volume up a bit.

"Carl," he whispered. "Come in."

The handset crackled and a voice came over. "Here."

"Location?"

"In a field directly behind the house."

"Good. I'm breaking in through a cellar window in the back of the house. Follow me in."

"Loud and clear."

"Remain radio silence."

Don't hesitate. Just act.

Detective Lane turned down his radio and placed it back into its holster. He took off his blazer, wrapped it around his arm, and elbowed the small window. Shards of glass fell inside and shattered against the floor. With his gun, he cleared the window so he could climb in. He peered in, and after a few moments, he climbed through, feet first. Once inside, he put on his coat, but before he could insert his second arm, something crashed into his face. The crunch of cartilage came at his ears. Pain exploded in his nose.

And then he blacked out.

CHAPTER FORTY-FIVE

As Detective Lane climbed through the window, Aisha couldn't help him. Not because she was riddled with pain from a possible broken rib and a fractured arm; it was because she was gagged and bound to a metal support beam. Her head reeled. Her ribs shot fire with every breath. She sat on the dirt floor and watched as he slid through feet first, a sliver of moonlight spotlighting him. He didn't see the figure walk up to him as he put on his coat. She saw the figure. The crack of the detective's nose caused her to flinch. His body thudded to the floor. His weapon next to him. A chuckle filled the room.

He lay there waist up in the moonbeam. Face covered in blood. Then his body slid out of the light and into the dark, dank basement.

"Take the time to paint the windows black and what do you get for it? A busted window," said a young man's voice.

"Or nose," said another male voice.

This one was older. Elderly.

Familiar.

"Tie him to the chair," said the older voice.

CHAPTER FORTY-SIX

A gradual orange glow flickered and filled the room. Shadows danced across the walls. Aisha peered over her shoulder and winced at the pain in her side as she tried to see who else was in the room, to see the two men. Someone came into her peripheral vision. She turned the other way. Uncle George picked up the detective's gun.

"Won't matter that you know," he said, sticking the weapon into the front waistband of his pants.

He leaned in and pulled down her gag. Goggles of some sort dangled from his neck. "Fancy, huh? Know what these are?" he said, leaning back up. "Night vision. Like being a cat in the dark. Can see anything."

"Can buy anything on the internet," said the young voice from somewhere behind her.

"George? Wh–what's going on?" Aisha said, confused, and pulling against her restraints. "What are—" She winced from the pain in her side. "What are you doing?"

George ignored her and walked away, out of her view.

"Use the nice detective's walkie," said George, "and see what the situation is."

"Gotcha," said the other voice.

"Detective Lane? Where is he?" Aisha said, trying to peer over her shoulder.

"Come in. You there? Come in."

Static.

Then a voice crackled through the walkie. "Here."

"Is the pig in the pen?" said the younger voice.

"Everything's fine as swine."

Aisha didn't know whose voice spoke on the other end of the walkie. She knew it wasn't Detective Haines, though.

"That was a clever one," said George.

"It was." The younger voice chuckled.

The voice crackled from the walkie. "What do you want me to do with him?"

A moan from Detective Lane interrupted the conversation.

"Waiting," came the voice from the walkie.

"Hang on," said the younger voice coming from behind Aisha. "What's the word?"

George stepped back into Aisha's view and stared at her for a moment, then said, "The detective will wanna hear this. Help him along."

The sound of a slap forced Aisha to look back over her shoulder. She tried not to give the pain any attention, but it let her know it was there.

"Ya awake?" said the younger voice.

"My–my nose." said Detective Lane, his voice nasally. "Where...where am I?"

"At the goddamn Regency," said George. "You cops were never smart. If you were, I wouldn't be standing here."

"Detective?" Aisha said. "Detective? Can you hear me?"

"Huh?" said the detective.

"It's me. Aisha Jones," she said. "Who's with you?"

"You remember where you're at now, Detective?" said George.

"The farm? House... Benjamin." A pause. "Darren."

The moment Aisha heard the names, she pulled against the ropes. Pain be damned. Her son and boyfriend had escaped her thoughts, and the detective reminded her of why she was in her situation to begin with. To save them.

"Get on the walkie and tell him to blow the house down," said George. He looked at Aisha. "I'd stop if you want to see your son again. Or Ben."

She paused, her breathing labored, and as she sat there the pain came back twofold.

"I want the detective to hear this," said George. "Tell him."

"Your orders are to huff and puff," said the young voice. "Blow the detective down. And we wanna hear it too."

The walkie-talkie crackled. Not a voice or word spoke as the moment hung in the air like the *tick tick tick* of a time bomb. Apprehension filled Aisha. She didn't know what to expect, but whatever it was, her nerves told her it wasn't good. Aisha closed her eyes.

Pop! Pop!

She hung her head and tears fell onto her lap. She didn't know Detective Haines. She knew of him, that was all. He attempted to save her son and Benjamin. He paid the ultimate price, and all she could do was cry.

The voice came over the walkie. "The piggy's been put to pasture as ordered."

"Tell him to bring the boy."

"And Benjamin?"

"He can wait. He's not going anywhere."

"Come home, and bring the boy," said the young voice.

"On my way. Over and out."

A soft sobbing came from behind Aisha. She didn't need to look to know whom it came from. She kept her head down and continued to cry with the detective.

CHAPTER FORTY-SEVEN

Before Benjamin splashed the front of the house with the gasoline and poured a trail back into the barn, he swung at the floodlight above its entrance with a shovel. After his second attempt, the bulbs shattered, glass raining on him. He wasn't sure if his kidnapper, and the killer, was inside the house, but he couldn't afford to be seen. If the person was inside, then he or she would be forced out by the fire through the front door, which he left untouched by gasoline. Or the person would die.

He dumped the rest of the gas throughout the barn save for the trapdoor. He didn't want the sheriff to go up in flames. He knew he couldn't pull him out. He was too heavy for that, but he was sure his body would remain untouched since he was below, in the earth. Ironic, he thought, the sheriff's own grave would be the one thing that would protect him. He tossed the can onto the floor, closed the hatch, found a screwdriver lying on the ground, and placed it into the latch. He dug into his pocket and pulled out a small box of matches.

With one swipe, it lit.

He tossed the match as far from him as he could, hurried out of the barn, and watched flames explode into a frenzy and spread. The slam of what he thought was the front door pulled his attention to the house. He glanced around and saw no one. He scanned its windows. Nothing. No movement. Was it the door? A streak of fire raced past him along the ground. He ran to the driveway. When he was far enough away, he stood there and watched the place that held so many secrets burn. The man he called Dad, the man he loved, would die a second time. Benjamin smiled. The flames licked the side of the house, savoring every inch as it grew. His forgotten childhood hissed and snapped and swirled into smoke and dissipated into the night.

Benjamin couldn't bring back the children. Or Tyson. Or the sheriff. But setting fire to the place that took them would release them.

Cleanse him.

Free them.

A new start.

A new life—

A woman screaming, "Noooo," cut through the growing bonfire. In an instant, Benjamin realized there were others in the house. Then his heart plummeted.

"Aisha!"

Oh god.

"Darren!"

He spotted the shovel lying among the broken bulbs of the floodlight, snatched it up, and raced toward the house. The flames nipped at the second-story windows. Without a thought to the hell around him, he tapped the screen door handle. It was warm, but too hot to grab hold of. With the blade of the shovel, he pried open the screen door and held it out of the way with his foot. He didn't give the doorknob of the front door a chance and crashed the spade down onto it. Again, he slammed down. It broke off and rolled between his legs.

Pop! Pop!

That was a gun. Jesus.

"Aisha!" He kicked the door, but it resisted from opening.

Pop! Pop!

In one swift motion, Benjamin rammed his shoulder into the door and he fell in, shovel gripped with both hands.

CHAPTER FORTY-EIGHT

Footsteps came down the basement stairs. Darren was in the arms of a young man. A sheriff? A shot of adrenaline straightened Aisha's posture, excitement in her smile. Her son's duct-taped mouth and bound ankles shattered her moment of hope. His eyes were wide, puffy, and wet. Dirt streaked across his cheeks.

"Darren. Sweetheart!" She pulled at her ropes. "I swear—"

"Threats won't help you," said George.

The man set Darren down next to her. Aisha glanced at his silver badge and read his name tag. He stood and straightened his uniform. She leaned toward Darren; his wrists were tied behind him. She leaned back and sobbed.

"Couldn't have taken off his gag? Huh, *Deputy Travis Rudnick?*" Her words spat venom. "Is this how you serve and protect?" she cried. "Kidnapping children?"

From behind, Detective Lane said, "Where's the sheriff, Deputy? You couldn't get hold of him because you killed him, huh?"

"I do what my uncle says," Travis said.

"You ever kill a child?" said Detective Lane.

The deputy glanced at Darren.

"I'll kill you." The words shot from Aisha's mouth. "Straight up."

"If anyone's doing any killing, it's me," said the younger voice. "Deputy Redneck already had his fun."

"Take it easy," said George. "A tad eager, don't you think?" He smiled. "It's in your blood."

The deputy yanked Darren up and pulled his gun from its holster. "I'll do whatever is necessary to make my uncle happy. Even if that includes killing a kid."

It came from her gut. Instincts. Aisha gave it everything she had. All her anger, fear mixed into one loud scream. One word. "Noooo!"

Darren bawled. Tears seared their way down his face.

Uncle George chuckled. "You've sure made me proud, Travis." He turned back toward where Detective Lane was and said, "Don't let anyone ever tell you that you can't create a killer, Detective. Takes time, that's for sure. Gotta control them. Make all their decisions for them. Make them trust you. Rely on you. He's had abandonment issues his whole life. That's key in creating a murderer. And it started when I…borrowed…this boy from his mother many moons ago." He turned back to the deputy. "Halloween, I think it was, and now look at him."

Aisha could have sworn her heart stopped beating. She sat there, frozen. Breath held. She remembered him. The article, his article. She wanted to cry, but couldn't. Everything was too much anymore.

"What?" Travis said.

The look on his face told Aisha all she needed to know. It was of shock. His mouth open. Eyes squinted. Confused. He pushed Darren toward Aisha. She used her legs to catch him, and he fell into her lap.

"You didn't know?" said Detective Lane.

"You mean I'm not your nephew?" said the deputy, taking a step toward George, pointing at him. "You *stole* me?"

"Let's not get emotional."

"You kidnapped me?" He glanced down at Darren, tears brimming his eyes. He scratched his head with his gun. "You told me you raised me because my mother abandoned me. Are you even my uncle?"

"No, I'm not. What's it matter? I raised you as my own," said George as he held out his arms. "And you've done good."

"I–I don't even know who I am."

"You're a killer," said Detective Lane. "Because this man made you into one."

Travis looked down at Aisha. "Or…or who my mother is. Father." He then looked at Darren. "I did everything you said, because I was afraid you'd leave me." He aimed his gun at George. "And you've always beat that into me since I can remember. Threatened to leave me. That my mother left me, and that it was *my* fault. *You* said I made her leave!" He rubbed his hand over his face. "What's my last name? My *real* fucking last name?"

"Fletcher," Aisha said. "It's Fletcher."

"He's not my cousin? Holy shit!" said the other young voice as he stepped next to Travis. "Did you kidnap me too?"

"You're…you're the kid I saw at the ice cream stand," Aisha said.

He looked at her, night vision goggles around his neck, his Pioneers baseball hat atop his head.

"Point Park University," she said.

He tapped the bill of his ball cap. "Good memory," he said. "Yeah, I was in Mr. Cole's journalism class. You picked him up outside the school." He gave her a thumbs-up and smiled.

"Okay. Enough with the reunion," said George. "Richard. No, you weren't taken. You're my real son. This farm was going to be yours!"

"Did you kill my mother?" Travis said, taking a step closer.

"The best laid schemes of mice and men," said the detective.

George turned and pointed his gun at Detective Lane. "Shut up."

"Did you murder my mother?"

"You hear something?" Richard said. He went over to the basement stairs and went up them two at a time until he was out of sight.

"Often go awry," said the detective.

Pop! Pop!

George crumpled to his knees. Black holes blossomed in the center of his back. Blood soaked his shirt.

"Fire!" yelled Richard. He came bounding down. "There's smoke! The house is on fi— What the fuck? Dad!"

Travis turned to Richard.

Pop! Pop!

Two holes sprouted into Travis. One in his back and the other in the back of his head. He dropped to the floor.

Travis' gun landed at Richard's feet. He grabbed it and ran up the stairs.

"I did." George dropped his gun and collapsed onto his back. "I always...killed those who–who got in...the way."

Upstairs, the sound of crinkling cellophane grew louder.

CHAPTER FORTY-NINE

The house cracked, snapped, and moaned from the flames that engulfed it. Heat slapped Benjamin's face. Black smoke filled the living room. He pulled his shirt over his mouth and stayed low. With the shovel in his hand, he began army-crawling through the burning room when a pair of feet kicked into him and someone tripped to the floor.

He rolled onto his back and saw a young man looking back at him. The Pioneers ball cap caused him to stare hard at the man who was wearing some sort of goggles around his neck, gun in his hand. The young man's dirty-blond hair reminded Benjamin of...

Never thought I'd ever consider journalism as a major.

"Richard!"

Not if I see you first.

The young man's eyes grew wide, and then squinted. He coughed.

"What's going on, Richard?"

"In the basement." He scrambled to his feet and ran out of the house with his hand over his mouth.

Benjamin let go of the shovel and crawled faster toward the kitchen. When he got to the frame of the doorway, a crash came from behind him and he held his arms over his head. He lowered them. Half of the living room ceiling fell in and blocked his exit.

He knelt and crawled toward the basement door.

CHAPTER FIFTY

Smoke filled the dank room. A crash came from upstairs. The roar of the fire sounded closer as Aisha pulled her son in with her legs and squeezed him as if she were hugging him. She closed her eyes.

"Looks like this farm's...gonna bury all of...us," said George. He coughed. "Ya got any last words...best to say 'em now."

"Why?" said the detective. "That's the question we all want to know. Why kidnap all those kids? Murder?"

"Why did you raise Travis?" Aisha said, her eyes still closed.

George coughed, "Many...questions." He tried to force a laugh but only coughed again. "My dad liked...to do things to me...my brother. Loved us with...bruises. Pain. Manipulated...fear...a bastard...loved him...looked up to him. Wanted to be him...became him...wanted to...pass down...

"I got one," said a familiar voice. "Where's the two missing kids?"

Aisha opened her eyes. "Benjamin!"

He knelt before her and Darren, pulled the sheriff's knife from his pocket, and cut the ropes around her ankles and wrists. "Darren," he said, and handed Aisha the knife. He cupped his hand over his face and disappeared behind her. The smoke was thicker, the basement brighter.

"Glad...you m-made it, Ben," said George.

"You okay, Detective?"

"Yeah."

As Aisha cut Darren loose, he didn't move. His body was limp.

"Kneel to the floor. You too, Aisha," Benjamin said from behind her. "You and Darren keep low and cover your mouths. Crawl on your bellies."

"Sweetie?" She pulled him up. "Darren? He's not moving!"

Benjamin and Detective Lane crawled over to her. "Let me see," said the detective. He pulled the boy's shirt up and put his ear to his chest. He gripped Darren's wrist and stared at Aisha.

"Is he?" she said.

Benjamin grabbed her hand.

"No," said Detective Lane. "He's breathing. We got to get him out of here."

"The window," Aisha said.

Instead of crawling, they ran to the window. Benjamin carried Darren while Aisha held the back of his shirt. Detective Lane led the way.

Benjamin handed Darren to Aisha. "You go out first, Detective." He bent over and cupped his hands together.

A dress shoe stepped into Benjamin's hands and he lifted the detective, using his legs to push him up and out. He hunkered next to Aisha.

"Give me Darren," yelled the detective.

Benjamin grabbed the boy and raised him up. A moment later, Darren's little legs disappeared through the window. He knelt down to Aisha. "C'mon." She stepped into his cupped hands and he lifted her up. "Hurry."

Once she was out, Benjamin lay on his stomach and crawled over to George, who lay still, his breathing short, slow.

Through his cupped mouth, he said, "Unc— George." He shook him. "George?"

"What are you doing?" yelled Aisha.

The smoke was thick, and it filled the basement like black cotton. Benjamin couldn't see her when he hollered, "I'm coming!"

A loud smash came from upstairs.

"George?" Benjamin said.

The old man coughed.

"C'mon, George. Get up." Benjamin hacked into his hand. "I can't drag—"

"I'm not...g-going any...where," said George.

"Get the fuck out of there, Ben!" said the detective from the window. "Hurry!"

Benjamin pulled himself to George's face.

"I tried to save you. That's the difference between your kind and me. I tried to *save* you. Not take your life."

"That's...because...my brother was weak...always was." George coughed. "Why he...hung himself...weak...I...I should've...killed you long ago."

"You sure you," Benjamin coughed, "weren't the weak one?"

George chuckled as best he could.

"Only losers...take themselves out...life is unfair for losers...like you...and your dad."

"He's not my dad! And I'd rather be a loser than be you or him."

"Benjamin!" hollered the detective.

"I'm coming!"

Benjamin covered his mouth and army-crawled back toward the window.

"Ben?" said George. "B-Ben?"

He paused and looked back. Smoke surrounded the old man save for his legs.

"Yeah?"

"Y-you and..." He chuckled, and then it turned into a coughing fit. After a few seconds he continued. "You're one of...the m-missing...missing kid."

The old man's legs faded into the black cloud as if a shroud enveloped him.

"Where you at, Ben?" said the detective.

"R—right—right here."

He continued to the window, held his breath, and stood with his arms upward. Seconds later, he felt the detective grab him by the wrists and lift him out of the basement.

? ? ?

Aisha held Darren in her arms in the field behind the burning house as Benjamin came up to them. Her face was black with soot and wet with tears, aglow from the fire.

"We need to get him to a hospital," said Detective Lane. "My car is parked not too far from here. I'll go get it." He grabbed Benjamin by the shoulder and led him away, and whispered, "He could have brain damage. Permanent damage. I'm not sure how long we were in there with all that smoke, but..."

"Go," Benjamin said. "Hurry."

As the detective ran off, Benjamin put his arms around Aisha and Darren and gave them a gentle hug. She leaned her head onto his shoulder and released soft sobs.

"I thought maybe I lost you in there," she said.

"You can't lose me that easy."

CHAPTER FIFTY-ONE

Eddie's unmarked Malibu came into view underneath the moonlight as he ran down Coal Run. It was parked off to the side of the road, against some trees. He pulled his keys from his pants pocket as he stopped at the driver's door and fumbled for the right one.

At his back, something pressed against him.

"Anything funny, and I'll put a window in your back. Raise your hands."

"Anything you say." The kid's reflection was in his driver's window. His baseball hat sat crooked atop of his head. "Richard, was it? That's your name, right? Richard? You don't want to throw away your bright future, do you?"

"Kinda past that point," Richard said. "Open the door, slowly."

"You don't want to shoot a detective, son."

"Try me," Richard said. "Open the door."

Eddie unlocked and opened the door. Inside, the dome light came on. "Now what?"

"Without turning around, I want you to hand me the keys over your left shoulder with your left hand, then get in behind the wheel and shut the door."

"You sound like a bright kid. Are you sure—"

The object in his back pushed harder.

"Just do it."

"Okay. Whatever you say. You're the boss."

Sirens wailed off in the distance. Down the road, toward the farm, pinpricks of red and white lights blinked.

"Firefighters," Eddie said.

Thank god.

"They won't be saving much," Richard said. "Keys."

Eddie had his share of fights. He never once sucker punched anyone. He fought fair. No guns at knife fights. No five against one. It was *mano a mano*. And it was time he broke his own law, just this once, and hit someone when they least expected it.

"I meant to ask before. Are you the one who snuck up on me and busted my nose?"

Richard chuckled. "Yeah. Popped you a good one, huh?"

"You did," Eddie said, as he inched his right foot forward for balance and leverage. "Good one is right."

He held up the keys with his left hand as ordered and passed them over his left shoulder. As soon as Richard's hand touched his keys, he dropped them. In one motion, Eddie spun to his left while he swept his left arm down and across, knocking Richard's gun hand away while he brought his right fist up and punched him square in the nose.

The break in Richard's nose sounded like a dry twig snapping under foot. He stumbled back into the trees and fell, disappearing into the darkened shrubbery.

CHAPTER FIFTY-TWO

Out the square window in the back door of the ambulance, Benjamin watched the road roll away. Lights flashing against it. Sirens greeting the break of dawn.

Y-you... you're...

That's the difference between your kind and me.

...one of... m-missing...

I tried to save you.

...missing... kid.

Not take your life.

Kid.

"Hey," Aisha said. A gentle nudge came at his ribs.

"Huh?"

"You all right?"

The paramedic held an oxygen mask over Darren's mouth and nose as Aisha held his hand.

"Yeah, I guess. You?" Benjamin said.

"Okay."

He turned back to the window.

"What took you so long to get out of the basement?" Aisha said.

"Wanted to give him a chance."

"At what? Life?"

"Not sure."

"Wanna know something?"

"Huh?" he said.

"The deputy? He was one of the kidnapped kids."

Benjamin turned back to her. "Really?"

"You remember the article we found with the little boy who was taken on Halloween? Travis Fletcher?"

"That's him?"

She nodded.

"Wow."

He glanced at Darren and thought for a moment. Until George gave him the news, the last thing he'd ever expected was that the two missing bodies weren't actually missing, lost, or dead, but rather, alive. That the missing kids—Travis and himself—were living out normal lives.

"Travis didn't take the revelation too well. He's the one who shot George."

"I don't even remember seeing Travis in the basement."

"It was crazy. Things just…happened. Really fast. I hope none of us remember it."

The scared look on Richard's face popped into Benjamin's mind.

"Richard," he said. "He tripped over me in the living room when I was crawling on the floor. He ran out. He's still out there."

"Detective Lane knows about him," she said. "I'm sure he'll be caught in no time."

For a moment, the siren filled the silence between them until Benjamin said, "Richard's not the other missing kid."

"I know. He was George's son. *Real* son—" Aisha's brows furrowed. "How'd you know?"

Benjamin cleared his throat. He tried to fight back his emotions: the anger, sadness, shock. The questions balled up in his stomach to the answers that tore his heart into two. "I'm–I'm the missing…" He bit his lip as tears boiled up. "Child."

Without saying a word, her face scrunched, and she hugged him and wept.

"I'm scared," he said.

Through blurry eyes, the paramedic looked over at him. "Is everything okay?"

He nodded in response, closed his eyes, and let the wail of the siren take him away. Far from Bradford. Miles from Pittsburgh. Somewhere far off, where he could run from himself.

"I'm scared of not knowing." Benjamin opened his eyes and stared at Darren. "Who am I?"

Aisha pulled away and cupped his face, her wet eyes locked onto his. "You're a sweet, caring man. That's who." She wiped her face. "A man who risked his own life to save me and Darren. You crawled through hell without a second thought." She sniffled. "*That's* who you are. And don't you *ever* forget it. Hear me?"

He nodded.

"I love you no matter what." She wiped beneath his eyes with her thumbs. "I don't care who you are, because *I* know who you are."

CHAPTER FIFTY-THREE

Benjamin woke to the sound of a flushing toilet. He rolled over and found Darren next to him, sleeping on his back. The bathroom door opened, and Aisha came out in pink pajamas. She wiped her eyes with her palms and slipped beneath the sheets on the other side of her son.

"What's the matter?"

"I'm fine," she said.

"Sure?"

She leaned over Darren. "Positive."

He propped himself up on his elbow, and they kissed. They lingered, and he soaked her in.

"Ewww," Darren said.

Benjamin pulled away and laughter bubbled up around them.

"Good morning, sweetheart," Aisha said. She gave him a quick peck on his forehead and lay on her back.

Darren rolled onto his stomach and rested on his forearms.

"How you feeling, buddy?" Benjamin said.

"Can we have pancakes for breakfast?" Darren said.

"Sounds good to me. How about you, honey?"

"Do you want IHOP's pancakes?" she said, and flipped onto her side to face them.

"Yeah, let's go to IHOPS," Darren said.

"Then pancakes work for me," she said.

Benjamin turned his back to them, opened the nightstand drawer, and pulled out a folded handkerchief. "But first let's play a game." He pushed the drawer back in, rolled over, and sat up.

"What kind of game?" she said, sitting up.

"Gotta play to find out," Benjamin said.

With the handkerchief tucked into one of his palms, Benjamin held out his balled-up hands to Darren and said, "Pick one."

Darren pointed at his left hand.

Benjamin gave him a smile and a quick nod, rolled his hand over, and opened it to an empty palm. "Sorry, bud. Nothing."

"You try, Mommy," Darren said.

He moved his right hand to Aisha.

She looked at him and gave him a sly smile.

"Go ahead," Benjamin said.

Aisha tapped his hand.

Benjamin rolled his hand over and opened it, revealing the handkerchief.

"Open it," Darren said.

She unfolded it and inside sat a diamond ring.

Aisha's eyes widened. A grin spread across her face from ear to ear. "Is that?" Tears filled her eyes. "I'm already crying." She giggled.

"Yes, it is," Benjamin said.

"It's a ring, Mommy. Don't you like it?"

She wiped her eyes. "I love it, sweetie. It's beautiful."

Benjamin thumbed his eyes.

"Why you crying?" Darren said.

"Because I'm happy." He rubbed Darren's head. "What would you think if I became your daddy?"

"Yeah! But...but my real daddy..."

Benjamin cupped the back of Darren's head with his hand and pulled him close. "I'll never replace your real daddy. Okay?"

Darren nodded.

"But I do wanna be your daddy. Take care of you and your mom. Be there for the both of you." Benjamin looked at Aisha. "And before my arm falls off, I should ask your mom first."

Aisha giggled through her tears.

"After everything, I've come to the realization that I want you and Darren in my life forever. I can't imagine living without you both. Will you marry me, Aisha?"

"My answer has always been yes." She grabbed him and hugged him. Without looking, she tugged Darren into the mix.

Hogarth lumbered into the room and barked at the excitement.

Benjamin pulled free, grabbed the ring from Aisha, and placed it on her finger. She held out her hand and admired it. She kissed Benjamin. Darren made a sour face and climbed out of bed and ran out of the room, Hogarth galloping after him.

"Now I've got a game for you," Aisha said, then reached into the breast pocket of her pajamas and held up a white plastic stick.

Butterflies fluttered throughout Benjamin's stomach as goose pimples bubbled up his arms. "If it's positive, it'll be..." The hair on his neck stood. He smiled. "I hope it's positive."

"It's positive!" She laughed through more tears as they hugged.

"Darren?" he said. "Come here!"

"You're going to be a big brother, sweetie!"

Hogarth barked downstairs.

"Here," she handed him the pregnancy test, "I'll go get him."

Benjamin studied the plastic stick as he swung his legs over the side of the bed, sitting and wondering how his life was going to drastically change. Having Darren was going to be fun, but having two was going to be amazing. Chaotic and fun. As a household should be. But filled with tons of love. His future felt so alive at the moment.

"Darren! Ben! My baby!"

Benjamin tossed the test down onto the bed and sprinted downstairs, skipping several steps as he did. The front door was wide open. Outside, Hogarth barked. Aisha was kneeling on the sidewalk, a letter in her hand, crying. "Darren!"

"What happened?" Benjamin knelt and grabbed Aisha by the shoulders. "Where's Darren?"

Neighbors were coming out onto their porches.

Aisha pointed down the road.

An old red wagon, one that looked familiar, turned a hard right onto the main street and disappeared.

Benjamin sprinted, screaming for help. Pleading for the wagon to stop. Yelling, crying, for his future son. Crying for the world to listen to his plea. "Help!" His legs carried him as fast as they could as he ran, ran, and ran, and came to a stop. "Darren!"

Tears and anger filled his face.

Aisha, with her trembling hands over her wet face, came up and hugged Benjamin with such strength it nearly squeezed the breath out of him. He didn't want her to let go.

"What's...? What's the letter say?" Benjamin said, afraid to know.

Aisha pulled away, her face full of pain, and handed it to him.

"I-I don't know what it means?"

Benjamin opened it and, in black marker, it read:

"You ever feel so alone even in the company of another? That's me. Work was my life. And my life was work. Cousins Dan and George dead. Richard in jail. Sheriff dead. Deputy Travis dead. The family gone. But my new family has begun and my new son will grow up to be just like them. I'll teach him well. The thing about family is you can choose them. I always wanted a son, and now I have one. My wife never wanted children. She never had a care in her bones. May God rest her soul. But I'm not alone. Not anymore. Pigs are never put out to pasture. And Eddie, even in your company I

was alone, and I think you were too. Still are, I'd guess. You were a good partner. I'll be expecting you."

CHAPTER FIFTY-FOUR

Cincinnati, Ohio.
Thirteen Years Later.

While looking through the eye holes of his wolf mask, the driver pulled his old red wagon into the parking lot of a playground and parked in a spot nearest to the swing set, leaving the wagon idling. The area was surrounded by trees of various-colored leaves: reds, golds, and browns. It was hot under the mask, even with the window rolled down. The cool air gave no comfort. Sweat trickled down his neck as his nerves rattled. This was the wolf's first time.

There were three kids playing around the swing set. A girl and two boys. She was about fourteen. The other two were much younger. Maybe five or six. Twins. One boy was kicking stones into the lot while the other was being chased in circles by the older girl.

A distracted sitter was what he needed. Distractions, he was taught, always left a child vulnerable.

The boy kicking stones looked up and saw the red wagon.

The driver waved and motioned for the boy to come over.

The boy was smart and ran, yelling something to the older girl.

Without hesitation, the wolf threw the wagon into reverse, backed out, and left the three kids behind.

He removed the mask and swiped sweat from his face.

"You got this, D-Man."

A school-crossing sign appeared on the right. He lowered his driver's window a little more.

He slowed down when a middle school came into view. There were kids with their parents in the back, playing on teeter-totters, swings, and slides.

In the front of the school there was a young boy, about eight, sitting on steps that led to the entrance of the school. He was playing with a tablet. Distracted.

After pulling into the school's parking lot, the wolf parked the wagon.

The driver pulled the wolf mask over his face.
He would try again.
Until he got it right.
Until he made his dad proud.

ACKNOWLEDGMENTS

The book you have in your hand was completed in 2013. Twelve years ago! Back then it was called Coal's Run, which had a double meaning, and it was my thesis for my alma mater Seton Hill University. And back then, the final chapter of this book hadn't existed. That's all me.

During my time at SHU, this novel had many fellow students who read and critiqued it along its journey to completion. Chapter by chapter. Unfortunately, I don't recall who they were but know that I appreciate their help with heartfelt gratitude.

Two people who were instrumental in reading, critiquing, and helping me with this book were my mentors and professors, author, Scott A. Johnson and editor, William H. Horner. I cannot thank them enough for guiding me. Thank you.

I want to thank Scarlett R. Algee for her hard work from final edits to formatting, among other things. A literary wonder woman who was an amazing partner, and supporter, in this book. A thank you to Sean Leonard for the initial edits. Thank you to cover artist Mikio Murakami, who did an amazing job on capturing the many deep (symbolisms) aspects of the book. And thank you to Chris Payne of JournalStone Publishing for taking a chance on a book that dives deep into darkness.

And as always, you, the reader. Thank you. It takes two to tango, as they say, and without you this dance can't happen. This writer/reader relationship. It's special.

ABOUT THE AUTHOR

Sheldon Higdon is an award-winning author and screenwriter. He earned an MFA in Writing Popular Fiction from Seton Hill University and is a member of the Horror Writers Association and The Society of Children's Book Writers and Illustrators (SCBWI). His publications include the award-winning middle-grade novel *The Eerie Brothers and the Witches of Autumn* and numerous short stories and scripts. He lives in Pennsylvania. Learn more at www.sheldonhigdon.com.